NO COUNTRY FOR OLD AGENTS

NO COUNTRY FOR OLD AGENTS

THE AGENT OPERATIVE™ BOOK 3

MARTHA CARR

MICHAEL ANDERLE

DISRUPTIVE IMAGINATION

LMBPN Publishing
PMB 196, 2540 South Maryland Pkwy
Las Vegas, NV 89109

Version 1.00, February 2023
ebook ISBN: 979-8-88541-851-5
Print ISBN: 979-8-88878-182-1

THE NO COUNTRY FOR OLD
AGENTS TEAM

Thanks to our JIT Readers:

Dorothy Lloyd
Wendy L Bonell
Diane L. Smith
Christopher Gilliard
Dave Hicks
Jeff Goode
Jan Hunnicutt

If we've missed anyone, please let us know!

Editor
SkyFyre Editing Team

CHAPTER ONE

So many champagne bottles were opened at the wrap party for *The Players* that it was like being inside a bag of microwave popcorn. *The Players* was finished, and Katie was a First Arret intern again, so Norah assigned the young woman to keep an eye on Sid and Bitta and confiscate any Pink Fairy they tried to take.

"Tell Sid I'll drop him from the agency if he gives you any trouble," Norah said.

"What about Bitta?" Katie asked, face pale as she imagined scolding the infamous director. The dwarf in question was wearing a sheer beaded poncho that brushed the floor below her six-inch Louboutins. Under the cloak, Bitta wore a nude jumpsuit—hopefully. The director was deep in conversation with Oleander, the fairy assistant director. Now that her job no longer required a megaphone and a campaign of terror, she was smiling and touching her lips to a plastic Barbie shoe full of the ludicrously expensive whisky Marina had sent.

"Norah!" Duncan called. "Want a glass of champagne?"

Norah nodded. Duncan whipped out his wand and shot a burst of sand-colored magic across the room. It curled around the stem of a champagne glass, lifted it into the air, and serpentined it through the crowd, the fizzy liquid sloshing against the rim. Twice, the magic flickered when some dark-brown energetic imperfection interrupted the stream, but the glass righted itself and arrived in Norah's hand three-quarters full.

"Cheers to that little stunt." Norah took a sip of champagne that was only a bit flat.

Duncan, who wore a tank top that resembled several pieces of string haphazardly tied together, grinned.

"Did the digital marketing team talk to you about streaming tonight?" Norah asked. "Go live while everyone's relatively sober. By all means, celebrate, but I need you among the living tomorrow for your screen tests."

A bit of red wine sloshed out of Duncan's tenuously held cup. "I've been living in a hype house, boss. I know how to stream drunk." He sounded professionally offended. Over his right shoulder, a pixie from the costuming department dove head-first into a bowl of piña colada punch.

"I'm less worried about you than some of the others. Chop-chop, Dunker."

Duncan pulled his phone from his pocket. "I'm going to try magic on the stream today," he said. "I told my followers I was avoiding it to prep for being a non-magical human in *The Players*, but..."

"You'll do great." Norah pointedly sipped her champagne. "If you don't, I'll help you figure it out. You're more than a wand, Duncan."

He nodded, took a breath, and raised his phone, face transformed by a bright, apparently authentic smile.

"What uuuup! Dunker Bunker here! I'm streaming live from the wrap party of my first big film. Woooo-wooooo! I want to introduce you to the incredible artists I've been working with..."

Norah ducked away before he could rope her into his livestream.

Party food was arranged on a table in the corner, and caterers circled with trays, but both were neglected in favor of the flood of booze. The food wasn't nearly as good as Angelo's. Norah plucked a shrimp puff from the buffet table, took a tentative bite, and chucked the rest into the trash as Stellan rolled up beside her. He had gotten the monster guts out of his beautiful beard and had styled it in a new way. The auburn hair was as beautifully smooth as a board. It looked like he was wearing Jennifer Aniston's scalp on his chin.

Norah admired it. "How do you get it so straight? Some kind of newfangled dwarven iron?"

Stellan shook his head. "Irons damage the hair and create frizz. This is a Brazilian blowout. Something about coating the individual hairs with keratin."

Norah considered calling Katie over and having her schedule an appointment, but, seeing that the young woman was engaged in conversation with Bitta, she decided to leave the intern to her relentless networking.

"I'm texting you the name of my girl," Stellan said.

Norah glanced across the warehouse at the set, which they'd half-destroyed with special effects. "Now that we're done, what are you going to do with the monster prop?"

Stellan grinned. "The Academy Museum of Motion Pictures bought it. They're doing a creature installation. My guy is going to be next to the *original* Swamp Thing." He said this as if it had some deep religious significance. For him, it probably did.

"That's great, Stellan," Norah said. "Will you tell Bitta I said goodbye?"

"You're not leaving to *work,* are you?" Stellan asked, incredulous.

Norah shook her head. "Nope. Just meeting a friend."

As she descended into the tunnels below Los Angeles thirty minutes later, Norah slipped her arms into a new jacket. It was made of Oriceran plant-based leather that looked and felt like cow leather—if the cow had been raised on a cloud and fed a nonstop diet of fabric softener. The material was unbelievably soft and beautiful and was dyed a blue so dark it was almost black. The salesperson had insisted it matched Norah's eyes.

Nostril met her at the bottom of the elevator, arms crossed and feet planted in a wide defensive stance. The girl scratched at a new stick-and-poke tattoo on her arm, swollen red skin surrounding, ironically, a rune for protection from disease. Her septum piercing had been updated with a realistic pewter bat, next to which swung a tiny ceramic doll.

"I'm only here because Shay asked me to come," Nostril shouted over the sounds from a miniature Bluetooth speaker attached to one of her belt loops by a carabiner.

The music was ninety percent screaming, maybe ninety-five.

Nostril was wearing cutoff black jean shorts. Instead of wasting the leftover denim, the teen had cut it into strips and sewed it into a cage-shaped overskirt. Ratty but cool.

"Have you considered a career in fashion?" Norah asked, looking at the sewing project.

Nostril eyed her suspiciously. "Fashion is a tool of the Man to keep us afraid of ourselves."

Norah stroked the blue plant leather of her sleeve defensively. *It's so soft.* "Out of curiosity, what *isn't* a tool of the Man?"

"Death metal and body modification." Nostril tapped her Bluetooth speaker.

"Cool song." The music had changed to something that sounded like cats dying stylishly. It was...distinctive.

"Not if you enjoy it, it's not." Nostril peevishly flipped off the speaker. A final wail echoed down the long concrete corridor behind her. "Look, lady, what do you want?"

"I'm looking for a guy named UrbanWurm," Norah said. "He's a hacker, and I've heard he lives underneath Los Angeles."

"Who'd you hear that from?" Nostril twined a loop of her overskirt between chapped fingers.

The psychotic light elf who lives in my coffee table. "An informant."

"Never heard of any worms." Nostril shook her head so ferociously that the charms on her septum piercing rattled. She stuffed her hands into the pockets of her cutoffs and gazed with great interest at the scuffed toes of her Doc Martens.

Taking a deep breath, Norah reached inside herself to the knot of magic she'd received from an enchanted antique radio. Following the complex loops of the enchantment, she found the twist of magic that activated it and tugged a thread of blue gum eucalyptus magic.

Nostril's emotions hurtled toward her. Teenagers teemed with emotions and desires, contradictory and sometimes nonsensical. Norah took a moment to receive the burst of new information.

Nostril was protective of her community in the tunnels. She was also afraid. Her eyes, which were surrounded by thick lines of meticulously applied black eyeliner, bored into the sunburst tattoo on Norah's wrist. A current of desire, deep and swift, flowed from the teenager into the tattoo.

"If you help me find UrbanWurm, my brother will give you a free tattoo. Not a stick-and-poke. The real deal," Norah blurted. *He'll be furious, but he'll do it.*

Nostril's eyes widened, and her lips parted. "How big? I don't want some lame butterfly on my ankle."

"Whatever you want up to a full sleeve. Andrew makes magic ink, too, so his tattoos can move. The pirate and mermaid on his arms are engaged in an on-again, off-again thing."

"Sick!" Nostril's eyes widened as this image flashed across her still-developing frontal cortex. "He's not going to ask for my ID, is he? I can't get parental permission or nothing." When Nostril said that, a tidal wave of loss almost knocked Norah off her feet. She shut off her magic. Whatever other skills the young punk possessed, she was *very* good at hiding her feelings.

"No ID. Just ink."

Nostril made a big show of pretending to think about the proposition, then nodded, spun, and pushed through a nearby door. They ascended an escalator that carried them to a wide gray tunnel. Their footsteps echoed on the concrete as Nostril took them into the heart of the labyrinth.

The accessible tunnels were used for film shoots, but the two left these behind. As the overhead lighting faded, Nostril pulled to a stop. "You got a flashlight? Some batteries?" Nostril, apparently, was conducting an informal preflight checklist. Norah pulled a slim, bright-blue aluminum flashlight and a new pack of batteries out of her pocket.

Nostril flicked on the light she carried and strode into the tunnel.

First came a series of concrete tubes, then a wide, rocky cavern as big as a baseball diamond. Halfway across this, Nostril stopped. "Look, I don't actually know where UrbanWurm lives."

Norah paused, her breathing loud in the massive space.

"Even if we don't find him, I still want the tattoo. Because I'm helping you," Nostril added defensively.

Norah wrapped her arms around herself. It was summer, but not underground. "It's important that I find him. He... Some terrible people are trying to hurt my parents, and I think UrbanWurm knows who they are. So, if you're leading me on a wild goose chase…"

Nostril scuffed a silver toe in the dirt. Apparently, Norah's mention of parents hit a nerve.

"The Wurm is more a legend than a person," Nostril

said. "No one has ever seen his face. He wears a spooky mask. Someone told me what it was once. A tar-tardigard?"

"Tardigrade?" Norah asked. She'd seen magnified photographs of the microscopic animals. They were segmented like worms and nearly indestructible. You could put one in a vacuum, then rehydrate it, and it would pop back to life. Norah didn't think it was a coincidence that the hacker had chosen it as an icon.

"Yeah, a tardigrade. Anyway, people say he's a tech wizard."

"Do they mean that metaphorically?" Norah asked.

Nostril shook her head, and the safety pins clattered again. "I've seen him a few times. Sometimes people hold a big market here for the people living in the tunnels. There's food and blankets and stuff, but also a lot of technology. We call it the Junkyard. Anyway, one time, I followed the Wurm in his mask. They say he lives in an underground palace, and he's spliced into the electricity and stuff from the grid. I wanted to see how he did it 'cause maybe I could do it too, y'know?"

"Build yourself an underground palace?" Norah asked.

"Sure. So I followed him. It wasn't hard, because he was carrying all this stuff. Monitors and computer junk. Except later, he wasn't carrying anything." Nostril frowned as if she had encountered a mental block. "Then he disappeared. Stupid magic.

"I made a mark on the wall. I'll take you there, but I want a guarantee on the tat."

Norah, more than happy to waste her brother's time, agreed.

Nostril nodded sharply and marched toward a waist-high pipe near the exit from the cavern. The corrugated metal was four feet in diameter and had thick black liquid trickling down the center.

Norah frowned. *It's a good thing I'm handy with cleansing magic.*

The crawl through the tunnel was blessedly brief, then they descended into something like a mineshaft rather than an underground cavern. After a series of twists and turns, Nostril stopped at the wall and crouched to point out a symbol near the base—a puffy round head with a serrated circle for a mouth. It was a good first draft of a tardigrade.

"This is it. The last place I saw him."

"You're not going to leave, are you?" Norah asked.

"Not unless things heat up."

Norah took a breath and activated her magical sight, then glanced at the rough rock walls and floor. At first, she saw nothing, but then a faint gray glow in the distance caught her eye. She almost missed it because it was the same color as the tunnel walls. *Handy, that.* Striding toward the glow, Norah found a thin trail of gray magic that split in two directions at a fork in the tunnel.

"Left or right?" she whispered.

She heard the man approach, feet scuffing at the end of the left-hand fork. The bobbing circle illuminated by Norah's flashlight landed on a sliver of gray fabric as it disappeared around a bend in the wall.

Norah ran after it. Nostril was following since the girl's metal piercings clattered behind her.

She was keeping up but not gaining. The gray-cloaked figure kept a steady pace in front of her. It was clearly more familiar with these tunnels, which wound through a labyrinth. She lost a few seconds finding the glowing gray trail of magic at an intersection but managed to catch up on a long straightaway that finally curved into a dead end. Norah, breathing hard, sprinted at the figure, who backed up against rock.

"Stop!" She pinned the man in the beam of her flashlight. He only stopped because he had hit the wall.

Norah's wand was out. When the man went for the cylinder of wood at his waist, she shouted, "Freeze!" He did.

She saw him clearly. Average height, clothes in heather gray, worn but clean. He wore an old-fashioned dark elf cloak around his shoulders, warm if not stylish. He was wearing his signature mask, which was creepy in the dark. The black hole of the mouth opened to reveal a pointed, toothy maw.

"Are you UrbanWurm?" The mask nodded yes. "Get his wand," she told Nostril. The young woman crept over, retrieved the wand, and retreated behind Norah.

"Are you the one behind Dark Hound?" Norah asked, her voice harsh.

"I'm UrbanWurm." The man's voice was deep and slightly hollow as if he were reading from a script.

"A lot of people died because of that site." Norah nearly choked on the words.

"A lot of people died," the man repeated. Something was wrong with his voice. Norah, wanting to fire on all cylinders, activated her radio magic. Was the man afraid? Was he toying with her?

A jolt of fear hit her in the back. It came from Nostril. The teen had a tough exterior, but she was still a kid. The ferocity of that emotion contrasted with the dead air in front of her. The man in the mask appeared to have no emotions.

Everyone has emotions.

Norah turned the radio magic up higher, searching, waiting for a tendril of emotion to reach her. She got nothing.

"He's not human," she said. "He's not alive."

The gray cloak slumped against the rough rock as the man collapsed. Norah ran to him, her wand at the ready for either healing or defense, but the body was still.

She kneeled and reached for the mask, alert for movement. The lines of the tardigrade were well-crafted. When she ripped the rubber off the head, she gasped.

The emotionless figure wasn't a person. It was a robot. Little attention had been paid to the look of the face, which was a clear plastic mannequin head stuffed with wires and circuit boards.

"Whoa," Nostril murmured from behind Norah's shoulder.

Norah leaned closer. As she reached to touch the clear plastic face, there was a pop and a burst of heat as flames flickered along a bundle of wire. As the flames spread, the plastic melted, admitting more oxygen.

"Get back!" Norah stumbled away as the body burst into orange fire. The tunnel filled with heat and light as the gray clothes of the Wurm disintegrated to ash. Norah plucked the mask away before it could be destroyed.

"A self-destructing robot. Cool," Nostril said.

"A self-destructing part-magic robot," Norah corrected. "I think UrbanWurm put a glamour on it to make it seem like a human. That means it left a trail we can follow."

Because the magic was the same color as the rock, following it was more about feeling the magic than seeing it—a gut sense that something supernatural flickered across the stone. They navigated back to the fork where they'd first seen the robot. This time, they took the right-hand tunnel, which ran into a long and complex series of corridors.

After a very long time, including a fumbled change of batteries, Norah and Nostril came to a hatch in the ground.

"Is that an old submarine?" Nostril asked.

It was. Norah gripped the round door-locking wheel with both hands. When she pulled hard, nothing happened. No movement. No sound.

"Help me." Nostril joined her. The young woman was strong. Together, they finally heard an eerie metal-on-metal noise. Flakes of rust fell to the ground as they swung the heavy metal hatch open. Light spilled into the corridor.

As Norah opened her mouth to offer to go first, Nostril whooped and leapt feet-first into the hole. Norah had a horrible moment of imagining one of Nostril's many piercings catching on the edge of the hatch, but the punk waved at Norah from the floor below the short drop and disappeared into the House of the Wurm.

That was what it was called: the House of the Wurm. The name was announced on a welcome mat below the short ladder from the hatch.

"Welcome to the House of the Wurm," Norah read. "Slightly literal, but at least we're in the right place."

The first surprise was how green everything was.

Norah had expected a gray and lifeless space, glowing with screens and redolent with Mountain Dew. Instead, after her eyes adjusted to the brightness, she saw a twenty-foot waterfall edged by verdant moss and thick vines. The cavern was long, with high ceilings, and the cascade fell against the far wall, where a slit in the ceiling fed into a matching slit in the floor. The water fell slowly, diverted by a maze of rocky shelves housing cutting-edge computer equipment. The mist shooting off the water cooled Norah's face as she walked over to inspect the techno-botanical hybrid.

Small holes were drilled into many of the casings, and water trickled inside. Norah stuck her hand into the stream and gasped at the cold. A sharp, freezing pain raced up her forearm, and she retracted her hand.

"Powerful computers need cooling." Nostril stuck a dirt-crusted finger into the water and shivered from the cold. "Bumper...he's my friend. He has a sick drum set. Anyway, he built this mondo PC out of parts from the Junkyard. We play games on his system sometimes, and we huddle around it if it's cold. The thing sheds heat like a radiator."

Norah was sure normal computer equipment would be wrecked by water cooling, but this wasn't normal equipment. The processors danced with protective enchantments for resisting erosion and maintaining structural integrity. Low-grade magic but durable.

Near the top of the waterfall, a funnel collected a portion of the stream and fed it into a vertical pipe network along a wall alive with plant life. A neat row of miniature sunfruit trees marched across the highest shelf, the ripe fruit glowing yellow and producing enough light to illuminate the plantings below. A clever system.

Wiping mist off her face, Norah inspected the wall of plants. The light from the sunfruit trees was augmented by brilliant grow lights, illuminating tomatoes, cucumbers, and fragrant herbs. A cool vegetal smell wafted from an Oriceran mint hybrid nestled next to three husky marijuana plants. Nostril was edging toward those.

"Don't think about it," Norah said. Tattoos were one thing, but she drew the line at giving children drugs.

Orchids bloomed in the cool mist. Their stems wound around metal scaffolding or dropped from glass terrariums hanging from the ceiling. The orchids, more Oriceran hybrids, glowed with magic, and their petals curled into eerie shapes. Norah brushed the tawny sepal of the closest one, which resembled a lion, and jumped when its petals snapped closed on her finger.

Cables protruded from the waterfall-cooled equipment like hairs and fell to the cavern floor. There, they were tied into neat bundles as they wound their way to an expansive desk. Clearly, this was Central Command. Norah expected the office chair at the desk to be damp, but the air in this part of the cavern was unnaturally dry and ten degrees warmer. On the ceiling, runes for dehumidification were entwined with runes for heat. Norah spun in the swivel chair, admiring the neat living space ringed by bookshelves built from old pallets and plywood scraps. The three robots lined up near the hatch startled her, but they were all deactivated. Dead, waiting silicon. They were meant to lure people away from the Wurm's lair rather than play offense. She hoped. ·

"It might not get much daylight, but the rent is hard to beat." Norah flexed her fingers as she inspected the keyboard

"This place is sick," Nostril agreed, awe and envy in her voice. She plucked a ripe tomato from the wall and ate it in one bite, red juice dribbling down her face.

"I want to steal his data," Norah announced, voice firm.

Nostril chewed meditatively and poked at a bundle of cables. "The chances of you hacking into the Wurm's systems are subzero."

"Oh, I'm not going to hack into his system," Norah corrected. "Come on, help me detach all the cables."

An hour later, they dragged what appeared to be a long, robotic centipede back through the labyrinth of corridors. Fiddling with cables under the icy spray had leached the warmth from her body, and Norah's teeth chattered. Several data drives had been physically embedded in the rock wall, and she'd used the last of her energy to magically chisel them out.

The corridor sharply turned a corner, and Norah stopped to refresh the antigrav wards under the center of the floating train of equipment.

"I hope you have plenty of papers to hold down 'cause that's all this junk is gonna be good for." Nostril breathed hard as she pushed the centipede's caboose.

Norah grinned. The UrbanWurm might be smart, but because he was a hacker, he had planned for digital threats. No doubt the system was lousy with firewalls and data encoding. What he *hadn't* planned for were physical threats. Like, for instance, someone taking all his shit. A humble yellow sticky note awaited the hacker's return to his now-empty desk.

If you want your stuff back, meet us at the Griffith Observatory on Monday. 1PM.

She'd considered adding "come alone" but decided it was cheesy and, on a practical level, unenforceable. Besides, she didn't think the UrbanWurm would morph into an urban social butterfly.

CHAPTER TWO

Norah's hair, dark brown and board-straight, stayed much the same no matter what she did to it. Generally, that was a blessing rather than a curse, but as she checked her appearance in a furniture store window outside Frondle's apartment, doubt overtook her. Why couldn't she make it fall in soft waves like all her female clients could?

She hadn't seen Frondle since they had defeated the monster at Universal Studios, a battle Norah referred to as the Dino Dispute. He was taking his sworn oath to bring down Dark Hound very seriously, so he'd routed most of his recent First Arret business through Madge.

Today, Norah was Frondle's agent, not his love interest. It didn't matter how her hair looked. She checked the window again and smoothed a single strand of frizz before unbuttoning the top button of her printed silk shirt. Strictly professional considerations.

"Good morning, Norah." Frondle appeared behind her in the window's reflection. His normally sunny smile was formal, and when she went in for a hug, he blocked her by holding out a hand for her to shake. Because he was so tall, this put a good three feet of space between them. *Leave room for three or four Jesuses! Or would that be Jesi?*

"How's my ingénue? Ready for your big audition, kid?" Norah asked in a parody of an old-timey Hollywood agent. The corner of Frondle's mouth quirked up, which reassured her that they hadn't lost their groove.

"Let's go. I miraculously found street parking in your miserable neighborhood."

Frondle stared at the sun for a few seconds, a light elf quirk that made Norah want to shove a paper bag over his face. After a moment, his smile warmed. "I thought we could go sun-beaming. The weather is supposed to stay clear, and it will probably save time," he added quickly in a vague stab at professionalism.

Norah perked up. Sun-beaming was a light elf activity, a cross between a mode of transportation and a sport. It involved swinging across the sky on beams of light like Tarzan on his vines. Sun-beaming was hazardous in cloudy weather and had been the source of many teen elf injuries. It sounded dangerous and sexy.

"We certainly don't want to be late," Norah said. "How do we start?"

Before she finished her sentence, Frondle wrapped an arm around her and sprang dramatically onto the roof of a nearby panel van, setting off its alarm. Norah was about to stop the klaxon with her wand when her stomach dropped out from under her.

Frondle pulled a beam of light at an angle from the sunny sky and sprinted, pulling them into the open air. At the apex of their swing, he pulled out another rope of light and let go of the first. They hovered in the air for a perilous second before the tension on this next rope caught.

They spent the first few minutes climbing until they were hundreds of feet above Los Angeles. Air whizzed past them, and her hair floated behind her as the houses and buildings shrank to the sizes of Legos.

Norah spotted the First Arret offices for a half-second, then Frondle said, "Hang on!" and they hurtled toward a cluster of gray buildings south of Griffith Park. Seeing a roof rise toward her, Norah closed her eyes, convinced they were going to crash. Instead, they missed the roof by three feet and swooped back into the air, Frondle's free arm stretched toward the hazy blue dome.

On the one hand, Norah was on the verge of puking her breakfast acai bowl across a wide swath of North Hollywood. On the other, Frondle's body was close and amazingly warm, with sweat beading invitingly on his tanned skin.

"Woohoo!" Norah shouted as he caught another rope.

Aside from the three times Norah almost vomited, the only eventful movement of the journey was when they narrowly avoided a paparazzi drone hovering above George Clooney's Studio City house.

"We don't have drones in Oriceran," Frondle yelled. "However, we do have large carnivorous birds and very rude Arpaks."

Twenty minutes after they had first swung into the sky, the roof of the building that would host Frondle's audition rose before them. Norah dropped onto it with a thud, breathless and invigorated. Sun-beaming was an excellent transportation option in heavy traffic.

"That was fun," she said as Frondle took three careful steps away from her. Cool air filled the negative space between them.

"I'm glad you enjoyed it."

They gazed over the edge of the roof into the smoggy North Hollywood morning.

"How do we get down?" Norah asked.

One antigrav cushion and a heart-pumping dead-drop later, they were in. As Frondle checked in with the casting assistant, the hair on the back of her neck stood up. The room was full of triple threats but no real physical danger.

"Will you run lines with me?" Frondle asked, shoving several printed sides into Norah's face.

"Sure, but I'm cutting you off after two run-throughs. I want you to be loose for this."

Frondle nodded. His face, which typically alternated between happy and serene, was pinched. It was understandable that he was nervous. A lead role on a sitcom would be big for someone his age.

He was auditioning for *Green & Pointy*, a prototypical network sitcom about an emerald crystal person and an elf living together in Greenpoint, Brooklyn. Cheesy, but it was network TV and paid accordingly.

Norah contemplated the sides, then started to read her part.

"You can't eat that," she began.

"But this is a bodega!" Frondle's voice hit a note of naïve confusion. "Don't bodegas sell food?"

"That's not food. That's a cat," Norah read.

"You can't eat cats?"

"The bodega cat hisses," Norah stated. Frondle shied away from her, feigning fear.

"Nice." Norah flipped through the script. "Can you cry on command? I don't know if they'll ask you today, but it's in act three."

He paused, then a bright smile spread across his face. "I can cry on command."

"Are you sure? I can buy you an onion. There's an Erewhon two blocks away. I will sprint there, and you can cry the world's most expensive tears." The last produce Norah had bought from Erewhon had nearly forced her to take out a small business loan.

Frondle beamed. "I can do it."

"Okay, good."

Norah glanced over her shoulder, unable to shake the feeling of eyes on her back. A chestnut-haired dark elf narrowed his eyes at her and looked at his sides. It was a glare of competition, not intimidation.

Shaking her head, Norah turned back to the script. "Sorry, sorry. Uh, you can try eating the cat, but I don't recommend it."

"Fine. Then I'll take this magazine."

Norah nodded. "It cuts to you walking down the street, eating the magazine."

"Am I going to have to do that?" Frondle asked.

"Maybe, but no practicing. I don't want you filling up on the *New Yorker* right before you perform."

A tingle went up her spine, and she spun. There! A flash of movement—white fabric disappearing down a corridor.

"What's wrong?" Frondle asked.

"Nothing. Look, you're gonna do great. You're ready. I'll be back."

Instead of pursuing whoever was watching her, she walked up the hall with her back turned, returning an email to Madge and waiting. Two minutes later, the hair on the back of her neck rose. *Gotcha.* She slowly stepped around the corner and down the stairwell to the building's underground parking garage. Steps echoed some distance behind her, and it took an effort not to look.

Inside the garage, she picked up her pace and slipped behind an enormous lemon-yellow Range Rover. Hidden by this monstrosity, she pulled out her wand, pointed it at the floor, and drew a large circle. Filling it with cross-hatches, she sent the spell into the floor. Then she slipped out from behind the SUV, slowing her pace and pretending to reach into her pocket for keys. She hoped her stalker would take a different route. When the footsteps started again, she smiled.

"Argh!" a voice cried, and a bloom of satisfaction rose in Norah's chest. Her trap had been sprung. When she retraced her steps, she found a compact figure struggling against the crackling blue ropes of her magical net.

"Why are you following me?" Norah demanded as she cast an illumination spell above her prisoner. When the light hit his face, she gasped. "Angelo?"

Norah's grip tightened on her wand as the sturdy caterer disentangled himself from the last strands of the trap. Drawing on the shadows in the corners of the room, the half-drow raised a small protective shield over his head and heart.

"Norah, please! I want to talk."

"If you want to talk, pick up a phone. Don't stalk someone into a parking garage."

"I tried calling! You never answered."

"Because I didn't want to talk to you."

"Did you get my gifts?" Angelo asked, rubbing his hands together behind the shield.

"I threw them away."

Angelo clutched his heart, looking so crestfallen that guilt tugged at Norah's guts. "There are unicorn colts starving in Rodania, and you throw away my beautiful food?"

"I don't trust you. How would you feel if I tried to kill *your* parents?"

"I'd feel sorry about your impending death," Angelo said earnestly.

Norah growled in frustration. "Your father is responsible for serious smuggling operations between Los Angeles and Oriceran, and he has gone to nasty lengths to protect his business. Did you really not know?"

Angelo pulled two biscotti from his pocket and offered one to Norah. When she shook her head, he took a nibble.

"I've spent my whole life trying not to learn anything about my father's business. I knew... Well, I didn't know much, but without my father's smuggling, I'd never be able to get the ingredients I want. I'm an artist, Norah. Don't ask me to shoot the man who brings me my paints."

Dark Hound was still active, displaying a three-dimensional grid of assassination targets that included her parents. A red starburst glowed between the eyes of every witch or wizard who'd been killed. *I won't let that happen to Mom and Dad.*

"Innocent blood has been shed." Norah's knuckles whitened on her wand. "Not to mention the personal inconvenience. The crew almost mutinied when I fired you from *The Players*. The whining was unbelievable. 'Ooh, Norah, these croissants aren't flaky enough. Ooh, Norah, the new barista doesn't make my nonfat macchiato like *Angelo*. Ooh, Norah, what do you mean there's no paella night this week?' I barely talked Sinter out of going on a hunger strike."

Angelo smiled, then schooled his face into earnestness. "I've left my father's company. Many people declined to follow me. They are concerned about their personal safety. For good reason, maybe, but that means all my current employees are bold and fearless visionaries!"

"Or tortured depressives with death wishes."

Angelo considered this. "Maybe my saucier. He is obsessed with black garlic and squid ink. But the rest of them? Visionaries."

Norah relaxed her offensive stance and crossed her arms, prompting the chef to drop his defensive shield. "I don't know, Angelo."

"Please. Think about it. Also, accept my gift."

He pulled a flat box from one pocket. The six-inch square was made from jade and had dancing fish carved into the lid. Deciding this wasn't a trap, Norah opened it. Impeccably constructed sushi gleamed in individual stone compartments, topped by yuzu slivers and shiso leaves.

"How long has this been out of the refrigerator?" Norah asked, poking a piece of marbled salmon.

Angelo beamed. "Two weeks!"

As Norah was about to upend the box into the nearest

dumpster, Angelo pulled her hand back. "It's perma-sushi. It's a special process using Oriceran-grown fish. Shelf-stable for a hundred years. Go on, try a piece."

Norah had used up a lot of adrenaline that morning, and her mouth watered. She slipped the biggest chunk of salmon sushi in the box into her mouth. Tangy rice melted into buttery fish, underscored by a hint of acid.

Norah ate a second delectable piece. Another, and then a fourth. When the box was three-quarters full, she forced herself to replace the lid.

"You like it?" Angelo was grinning. The weasel knew the answer. "Open it again." His eyes glinted with mischief.

Norah opened the box. It was full again. Every piece of sushi she'd eaten had been replaced while the lid was closed.

"Perma-sushi." Norah stared at the box in awe.

"Good for a hundred years," Angelo removed a second box, this one pale rose quartz, and placed it on top of the first. "For a friend. Enjoy! I will be in touch." Pulling his keys out of his pocket, he sauntered over to a large van. The Domenico and Son logo on the side had been painted over with a single word: Angelo's. Norah respected the simplicity.

Heading back up the stairs, Norah ran into the casting assistant, a young woman named Dakota. They'd occasion-ally emailed about auditions.

"Norah! I was looking for you."

"Oh?"

Dakota glanced around the stairwell and lowered her voice. "It's about Frondle. It's…I don't know. Is he, like, a real client, or are you repping him because he's a magical?"

Norah, surprised, stepped back and grabbed the rail to keep herself upright. "I don't rep anyone I don't believe in."

"Sure." Dakota seemed uncertain.

"He's ready. He's got that *thing* you can't buy for a million bucks. The It-factor. Everything else can be trained, and he's training hard. Every time I send him out, he gets better."

Dakota nodded. "Okay. Good. He's got the look, but we weren't sure…"

"He's gold. Don't sleep on him."

Frondle was waiting at the top of the steps.

"You're done already?" she asked. That wasn't a good sign.

"They asked me to stay and read with the crystal people."

That was a good sign.

"You don't have to stay. If you're busy." A chameleon's bounty of emotions crossed his face.

If I leave, it'll be another three weeks before I see you. "I don't mind," Norah chirped. "After all, I'm your agent."

CHAPTER THREE

Norah had only gone to Frondle's audition because she was a good agent, and she was only going to his apartment because she needed to talk to his roommate. She had repeated that to herself so many times that it had to be true. Anyway, Frondle wasn't there. He was at his acting class, not that she had his schedule memorized.

Still, her heart skipped a beat when the door opened.

She apparently didn't have Frondle's schedule memorized since there he was, six-plus feet of Golden Retriever energy.

"Norah!" The light elf's face shifted like a mood ring between delight, distress, and wariness.

"You're supposed to be at acting class," Norah stuttered.

She sounded like she was scolding him for playing hooky. Abashed, he lowered his voice to a whisper. "Please don't tell Madame Bavano I don't have laryngitis. She's already made me cry twice during scenes from *The Importance of Being Earnest*. This week, it's Edward Albee." He shuddered.

"My lips are sealed," Norah said. "I actually came to see Castor. I hope he's ashamed of his behavior and is now using his puppetry for good." *Is good puppetry even a thing?*

"Oh. Castor doesn't live here anymore. Taerial and Ammath turned his room into a podcasting studio."

As if the word "podcast" were a horrible summoning spell, a wooden door opened with a thunk, and two dark elves popped into the hall behind Frondle.

"Do you ever rep podcasters?" Taerial asked. The drow woman was wearing an oversized sweatshirt as a dress, and her green eyes were wide under platinum baby bangs. Dyed, Norah was sure, because the drow was several decades from going naturally silver. Ammath, in a salmon-colored sweatsuit, poked his girlfriend in the arm with a terrified look, then ran a hand through his frosted tips.

"What she means is, we'd love to have you on some-time," Ammath said. "It's called *Blondes with Wands*. We interview witches and wizards about their wands."

"I'm not blonde."

"We're the blondes," Ammath explained.

"You don't have wands."

"Yeah, that's why we interview people. Here, have a coozie." Taerial materialized one from her silver fanny pack.

"Uh, thanks," Norah stuffed the foam cylinder into her pocket. Unfortunately, that revealed the top four inches of her wand.

"Ooh, blue gum eucalyptus!" Ammath gushed. "Very retro. Very cottage core."

Norah touched her wand protectively, tempted to

whisper encouraging words to it. "It's a good wand!" There was enough edge in her voice to make Ammath flush.

"If you enjoy it, that's what counts." The drow spoke as if Norah were an elementary school talent show competitor.

"Do any of you know where Castor is?" Norah flipped through six different potential excuses for getting out of doing the podcast. Okay, four polite excuses and two types of food poisoning.

"We have not kept in touch," Frondle stated primly. Norah didn't blame him. They'd nearly had their magic digested by the disgruntled screenwriter-turned-puppeteer's animated monster's antics.

"Would you like to come in?" Frondle took a half-step away from Norah.

"I have to find Castor. I'm going to try Sid's. See what he knows."

Frondle put a hand out for Norah to shake. "I understand. As always, it is a great pleasure to see you."

Taerial's eyes narrowed and moved from Frondle's extended hand to the bereft look in his eyes to the blush creeping up Norah's face. Before the drow could make more snide comments about her wand, Norah excused herself.

Driving north on the 101 wasn't as fun as sun-beaming. Her Prius didn't hold a candle to Frondle's warm embrace. The memory of those long arms around her inspired several vivid daydreams, which kept Norah entertained until she arrived at Sid's soulless box of an apartment complex. When she knocked on his door, she heard feet scuffling. Hopefully, Sid was putting on something other than unwashed sweatpants. A moment later, he opened the door.

A briny smell wafted from the apartment, and Norah wrinkled her nose. What had Sid been eating?

"I didn't think Hollywood agents made house calls."

"It's one of First Arret's many premium services. Along with not dropping clients who lie to us about the authorship of their screenplays."

She attempted to imitate the smile Garton Saxon might use on a piece of veal. Sid gulped. "Uh..."

"Where's Castor?" Norah interrupted.

Sid flinched and blinked. "Um. I don't know?"

She wasn't convinced.

"You're a writer, Sid. You should be a much better liar. Spit it out."

For good measure, she activated her radio magic and learned two things. One, Sid was eager to change the subject, and two, there was another person in his apartment.

"Who else is here?" Norah pushed inside, ignoring Sid's protests. The other person in the apartment was desperate to remain hidden, which, ironically, made him extremely easy to find.

After a search that lasted all of fifteen seconds, Norah towered over Castor, who was curled up behind the kitchen island. "You haven't answered my calls."

A laptop sat on the kitchen island above Sid's head. On the glowing screen, in twelve-point Courier, was a page of a screenplay.

"Oh, my God. Are you two *writing* together again?"

"I told you she'd be upset," Castor mumbled as he scrambled to his feet.

Sid crossed his arms and stared at Norah. "You kept reminding us that *The Players* was good because we had written it together."

Norah, who still hadn't gotten the monster guts out of her favorite scrunchie, scowled. "I meant that you shouldn't try to kill each other, not that you should get back together. This is the worst will-they, won't-they in the history of cinema."

"I think we're doing some of our best work," Castor announced.

On the laptop screen, Norah scanned an action line.

Flora (28, brunette, hot but doesn't know it) wraps her arms around Spud (a heart-of-gold screwup genius).

"Flora? *Flora?* Now, what does that rhyme with?" Norah asked.

Castor slammed the laptop screen shut. "It's not ready for eyes."

"I can see that," Norah muttered.

Sid's lip curled. "Besides, I'm sure you are focused on Frondle. Professionally speaking, of course." Passive aggression suffused his words.

What the hell? Norah had seen Sid politely professional, anxious, and terrified. She'd never seen him snide. *If people are going to gossip about me having a scandalous affair, I'd prefer to actually have it first.*

Was her unconsummated nebulous thing with Frondle common knowledge?

She sighed. "When it's done, I will happily take a look at your monstrous creative lovechild. Until then, I'm here about Cleo's hands." She sniffed the air. The pickle smell was stronger here. Coming from the trash?

Castor coughed and met Norah's eyes. She sensed embarrassment seeping out of him. "I can't do the hands."

Norah narrowed her eyes. "We had a deal."

"I know, I know. I'm not trying to back out, but I can't get the joints right. I can't get any of it right."

"He keeps building hands and trying to open pickle jars with them. The neighbors have complained," Sid explained.

"So far, I'm batting zero. See for yourself." Castor opened the lid of a nearby trashcan, and the smell of vinegar and dill grew stronger. Inside a soggy trash bag, uneaten pickles swam in brine between shards of broken glass.

"I told him to ask Lottie so he can wrap this up and focus on our writing partnership, but he's been dragging his feet."

"Who's Lottie?" Norah asked. Castor's face went sourer than the mess in his trash can. Groaning, he turned to Norah. "Lottie Reiner. She worked at the marionette theater for, like, forty years. Everyone who's anyone in the puppet game knows who she is," he added, disdainful of Norah's ignorance.

"You think she could help you with the hands?"

"Yeah."

"Ask her for help. As one of Variety's Ten Young Puppeteers to Watch, maybe you can, uh, pull some strings?" Norah grinned.

"People make that joke a lot." Castor's eyelid twitched.

Universe, save me from self-serious puppeteers! "You owe me."

"I can't ask for a favor from Lottie Reiner," Castor protested.

"Why not?"

"Because she's super mean, and Castor's afraid of her," Sid said.

The corner of a rectangular object dug into Norah's hip, and she had a sudden idea. "Have you considered bribing her?"

"We're not exactly flush with cash right now," Sid replied. It was true. After Sid's lies and Castor's cursed-marionette-eye installation had come out, they had agreed to accept a bare-bones rate for *The Players.* In exchange, the executives at Silver Lion studios had agreed not to send their most terrifying attorneys to skin the pair alive.

"I might be able to help with that." Norah pulled the second box of Angelo's perma-sushi out of her pocket. She peeked under the lid to make sure the fish hadn't gone bad or turned to mush, but every piece was perfect, so she handed the pink box to Castor. "Try this. Infinite sushi. It never goes bad."

"Ooh." Sid's eyes lit.

"Hands off!" Castor scolded, peeking under the lid.

"Try it," Norah urged. "The box replenishes every time you close the lid."

Sid had edged closer to the sushi. He and Castor sampled a few pieces.

"Infinite sushi," Sid whispered. "Do we have to give this away? We could open a food cart. Make a killing."

"No, you couldn't. Look, go ahead and gorge yourselves,

but after that, give it to Lottie. See if she can help. I love Cleo, and she deserves the best work that unrefrigerated all-you-can-eat raw fish can buy. Got it?"

"Hmm. I'll try talking to her, I guess," Castor grumbled.

"Great. And pick up your fucking phone. I don't like repping people I can't get hold of."

As she spun, Castor tentatively asked, "You're repping me?"

Norah sighed. "Yes. Congratulations. You're my first puppeteer."

Goddess help us all.

CHAPTER FOUR

Andrew's face was the color of his reddest ink. "When you said you needed my help, I didn't realize you meant giving underage children illegal tattoos."

"That's not fair," Norah protested. "I also need you to help me take down a secretive and extremely dangerous hacker. Besides, you'll like Nostril. She says body modification is one of only two things that aren't 'tools of the Man.'"

The tiny vein on Andrew's temple remained prominent but stopped pulsing. "That's common sense."

"Don't you want a cool teen to think you're cool too?" Norah goaded.

A tiny globule of Oriceran lobe-sap crackled in Norah's ear. Stan had given her the tree a few weeks ago, and the gummy pea-sized blob in her ear was her first harvest. As far as she could tell, the magical resin worked like a walkie-talkie, except it had a rotten leaves smell and made your ear sticky. Stan insisted that lobe-sap signals couldn't be blocked, but as she scratched her ear, Norah wasn't sure it was worth it. However, when her mother's voice came into her ear, it was clear and at the right volume.

"Nostril is a lovely young woman. You'll like her. Also, comm check. Can you hear me?"

"Loud and clear, Mom. Can everyone hear me?"

Andrew nodded. "I can hear both of you. This is the Needler, check-check."

A snort joined the chorus of voices.

"'The Needler?' You have a chance to pick a code name, and you choose the *Needler*? You can be lame if you want, but I'm not doing it. I'm on the trail below Griffith. This is Quint, by the way, in case any of you losers have forgotten. Can we wrap this up? Glesselda's meeting me for a hike in twenty minutes."

That explained why Quint wasn't wearing a shirt. Norah didn't trust the ancient light elf. After all, she had raised Garton Saxon. At least she'd pulled Quint out of his romantic funk.

"All right, let's do this thing," Norah ordered. "Take it slow, Andrew. Look around. Pretend you're a tourist."

She opened her car door and spent more time than she needed to at the kiosk, paying the observatory's extortionate rates. Then she stretched, admired the Hollywood sign, glanced at her trunk, and strolled across the wide green lawn in front of the building.

Their timing was perfect. They headed up the wide marble steps and under the building's iconic gold dome a few minutes before their appointed meeting time. Los Angeles had to be the worst city in the world for stargazing, but the observatory persisted.

Norah killed time perusing a new exhibit on the astrophysics of Oriceran. A pretty sundial the placard identified as a collaboration between light elves and dark elves as part of a peace treaty was on display.

"I guess you need both light and shadow for a sundial," Quint said, looking over Norah's shoulder.

It was five minutes after one, and UrbanWurm still wasn't there. Or rather, if he was there, he hadn't identified himself. Families thronged in the room, which was noisy for a museum and full of parents trying to interest their bored children in the finer points of astronomy. As the minutes ticked past, the room got more crowded. Clumps of people clustered around a tall cage in the corner of the room.

"Ooh, a Tesla coil!" Andrew cried. "I love those."

The air in the room was thick and had a sour buzz, but not from the impending light show. A docent came out with a microphone and started a spiel about electricity and magnetism. After a moment, the coil came to life, electricity crackling in impressive arcs. A rainbow neon sign in front of the coil glowed to life.

"Don't be jealous of the coil," Norah whispered to her wand.

"What was that?" Petra asked.

"Uh, nothing. Still no sign of the Wurm."

The electricity shooting off the coil got brighter. A spark crackled off the neon sign outside the cage. *That's not supposed to happen.*

"Something's wrong." As she spoke, the front panel of the Faraday cage shielding the Tesla coil disappeared.

"Oh, shit!" Andrew exclaimed as an arc of electricity shot toward a clump of confounded teens. Andrew dove and barely managed to push them out of the way. The arc punched a smoking hole through an interpretative sign, changing "Astrophysics of Oriceran" into "As s of Oriceran."

At least it'll be more popular.

Another crackling bolt shot out. Norah countered it with a shield an instant before it hit a baby stroller. The Pomeranian inside, whose fur was dyed purple, did not look appreciative. Another bolt of light broke a window, and sunshine flooded the room as the Los Angeles skyline became visible through the jagged hole.

"What the fuck was that?" Quint sounded panicked.

Norah's eucalyptus wand was a blur as she drew cross-hatches in the air, desperately trying to reconstruct a facsimile of the Faraday cage. However, the electricity punched through her magic faster than she could reconstruct it. She gave up and settled for keeping the individual arcs from hitting tourists. The room was three-quarters empty now and getting emptier as visitors sprinted for the exits.

"I can't contain it!" Norah shouted, so distracted that she failed to see a sparking bolt coming at her face.

Andrew cast a spell he'd cast a million times as an ornery kid and yanked Norah's feet out from under her. Marble swooped up to meet her face as the killing bolt whizzed overhead, setting an interpretative sign about electrical safety on fire.

Maybe I don't have to contain it.

Instead of stopping it, she could try to channel the

errant energy into a spell. It would have to be big. Really big.

With a deep breath, Norah prepared herself. Channeling this much power was like aiming a firehose. You had to stay in control.

Panting with adrenaline, Norah ran for the broken window, emptying her mind and picturing her body as a glowing blue funnel. As she jumped out onto the balcony, she waved her wand in a tight hook and pulled every spark of electricity from the coil into her body. The sensation of her every hair waving in contradictory directions momentarily distracted her from the excruciating pain.

Direct it, don't hold it, she told herself. Her target came into view.

The Hollywood sign had been built in 1923 as an advertisement for a real estate development. Its flat white forty-five-foot-tall letters marched across the scrubland in Beechwood Canyon.

Making eye contact, Norah sent the energy from the Tesla coil toward the sign. Tourists screamed in the distance as flashing electricity shot over their heads. Her wand wove as she wrapped blue tendrils of magic around it, coaxing it into the shape of a spell, acid rising in her guts as the electrified magic—or was that magic-ified electricity?—closed the distance to the sign. When the leading edge of the spell hit the H, Norah winced. If her spell collapsed, the electricity would fry her in milliseconds.

It didn't collapse. Norah clenched her teeth in triumph as the magic shot through the white letters, splitting into runes that fractured into spells and the symbols for clarity, awareness, and intelligence.

The pain disappeared as the magic flowed through her, power-washing her from the inside out. Electricity wrapped in a protective blue sheath flowed from her eyes, ears, mouth, fingers, and nostrils, blue shot through with glowing light. Black encroached on the edges of her vision, and Norah pushed it back. *Not yet.*

The stream of electricity thinned, dimmed by the power of her spell. It went from a stream to a trickle, then faded as Norah lost consciousness.

She woke up on the marble balcony, brought back to consciousness by the sensation of her dandelion-puff hair waving around her head. She ran a hand through it and felt a crackle of static.

"I think it looks cool," Andrew said. "You're a low-budget Medusa."

Norah sat up slowly, the movement producing a noise like crackling leaves.

Andrew took a step back. "You're still a tiny bit electrifying."

A spark shot off Norah's elbow, and she scratched it. "I'll consider that a compliment."

She looked at the Hollywood sign. She had cast a spell, no doubt about that. The power had gone somewhere.

"What. Exactly. Did you do?" Andrew asked.

On the side of Mount Lee, across the stretch of green-brown scrub brush, past gravel trails teeming with excessively attractive joggers, was the Hollywood sign. It seemed to be unchanged—for a second. Then the double Os in Hollywood blinked and looked around.

"What the fuck?" Andrew asked, alarmed.

Norah's expression settled somewhere between pride and terror. "I might have made the Hollywood sign the teensiest, weensiest, bit sentient."

No one had died, and she'd saved a critical piece of Hollywood history from being electrified to smithereens. Had she made the right choice?

Across the hillside, the O in Holly rippled, and a booming "Hello" echoed across the park. Norah raised a hand and waved. Alarmingly, the sign appeared to see her and its weird mouth moved again. Norah didn't believe her ears, but when the sign spoke again, she was forced to adjust her assessment.

"Mama?" asked the Hollywood sign.

Andrew's magical earpiece crackled. Norah checked her ears, but the gummy blob of lobe-sap had been blown out when she'd channeled the electricity from the Tesla coil. Andrew listened, then choked. He tapped it, and after a moment, he coughed wildly.

"What is it?" Norah asked.

"Mom says... She says she's always wanted more grand-children."

"Uh..."

"Also, she says she trapped the UrbanWurm in the trunk of your car."

Petra was waiting by Norah's Prius, eyes fixed on the hillside. She ignored the alarmed shouts from nearby tourists. "You were right about him hacking your electronic locks." The doors clicked open with an eerie whine.

Norah went to open the trunk, but Petra pulled her back with a dangerous gleam in her eye.

"Not here. Let's go back to your apartment. I want to be somewhere private for this particular unboxing."

The place was crawling with cops, but they were more interested in keeping people out of the observatory than blocking the exits. Still, the road to Los Feliz was choked with traffic, gawkers on the shoulders risking their lives to photograph the fingers of smoke rising from the hilltop. Norah stayed alert to any noises from the trunk.

Petra had trapped the UrbanWurm using a spell she'd modified from a dangerous old grimoire Norah had found at the Old Zoo. When the hacker had opened the trunk to look for his equipment, he'd been mesmerized by the spell written on the interior.

"Then I pushed him in!" Petra explained brightly.

He wasn't stunned. Theoretically, he *could* move if he wanted to. But he didn't want to because he was totally mesmerized.

"That's a nice trick," Norah said.

Hoofbeats on the asphalt turned out to belong to Pepe, who tossed his head in the late afternoon sunlight. He sniffed Norah's car, wrinkled his nose, and wandered lackadaisically away to nibble on a hydrangea.

"Is he supposed to be wandering loose?" Quint asked.

Norah stared at Pepe's slitted pupils until discomfort forced her to look away.

"I think he has a key," she informed him, lowering her voice.

"How does a *goat* have a *key*? He doesn't have opposable thumbs!"

Unwilling to solve that mystery, Norah opened her trunk.

At first glance, the man inside was identical to the robot she'd apprehended in the tunnels. He wore the same gray clothes and a duplicate of the tardigrade mask. Maybe it was one of the other robots? A check with her radio magic disabused her of that notion, however. The captive was human, though the mesmerizing spell had distorted his emotional currents. Most people's emotions were frizzy, with curling tangents and conflicting desires. Not the UrbanWurm. His energy and intention flowed smoothly into the spellwork written on the trunk. All he wanted in the world was to stare at it forever.

"How did *you* avoid getting mesmerized?" Norah asked her mother.

Petra grinned. "My eyesight is so bad without my reading glasses that I can't see the spell. The perks of old age, I guess." The wrinkles at the corners of her mother's eyes crinkled in a smile.

"Let's get him out."

"If we move him, he'll wake up," Petra warned.

Norah shot a stunning spell at the curled-up figure and pulled him onto the asphalt. He lay limply, but when Norah reached to pull his mask off, the body exploded into motion.

He was an angry tornado, rolling across the ground behind a parked car as his hand flashed for his wand. The wood had been augmented with LED lights and etched gold lines like a circuit board.

Then he was on his feet, running. Andrew pointed his wand and pulled the Wurm's feet out from under him with a thread of green magic, sending the hacker flying head-first into a cluster of purple hydrangeas. Pepe, his snack-time disturbed, strolled over, kicked the cybernetic wand out of the hacker's hand, and took a huge bite of it. It snapped neatly in half.

The Wurm howled and tried to roll, but his upper body was entangled with hydrangea stems. Pepe summarily kicked his kneecap, which distracted the hacker long enough for Quint to pull him out of the bushes and yank his mask off.

Without the eerie mask, the Wurm seemed smaller. His skin was a deep reddish-brown, and his intelligent eyes scanned the scene for openings and opportunities. The second the mask was off, Norah zinged him with a stunning spell.

The Wurm fell on the grass, and Norah retrieved his mask. Its exterior was identical to the one she'd pulled off the robot, but the interior was more complex. The leather was imbued with a powerful anti-stunning spell, and Norah would have bet money that the Wurm's heather-gray cloak was similarly enchanted. Norah released the stun on his lips, and he sputtered with anger before her wand was back in her pocket.

"How did you trap me? I was shielded."

"We didn't trap you. You trapped yourself," Petra informed him. "And don't worry. That's not new-age bullshit. It's a tricky mesmerizing spell. If you're as smart as I suspect, I'm sure you can work out the details."

The Wurm growled, eyes burning with anger, "Where's my equipment?"

"Behind a firewall," Norah said, then relented. "Okay, it's not *behind* a firewall, but it's with a fire elemental who could raise a flaming barrier very quickly if she wanted to."

"Are you talking about Hazel?" Quint's voice was strained. "Have you seen her?"

"Way to blow the location of our secret cache, Romeo," Norah said. Quint's mouth shut with a rapidity approaching the speed of light.

"Who's Hazel?" the Wurm asked. His voice was very flat as if he weren't used to using it with other people.

"None of your business. Look, unless you want your gear deep-fried in lava, you better start answering our questions."

Pepe bleated encouragingly and licked the Urban-Wurm's cheek.

"Is that a goat?" he asked, wincing.

"As far as I can tell," Norah said. "If you tell me what you know about Dark Hound, I'll tell the goat to stop."

Sensing his window of opportunity closing, Pepe licked faster.

The Wurm blinked slobber out of his eyes, but the frothy goop failed to cool his temper. "Dark Hound? You're holding my life's work hostage over some lame fantasy role-playing game? What are you guys, rival game developers?"

"What?" Norah asked. Petra shooed Pepe away and leaned over the Wurm's face.

"Recognize me, bud?" she asked.

"No," the Wurm said flatly.

Norah pulled up Dark Hound on her phone as Petra leaned closer. Within seconds, a three-dimensional grid of glowing red faces popped up in the air. Petra raised her wand and poked the image of her face.

"Does this look like a game to you?"

The Wurm looked from Petra to the image and frowned. "I don't get it. You modeled for one of the characters?

"Characters?" Petra asked, and her voice was thin and cold. She poked more images with her wand, the ones identified with the red starbursts. As she touched each one, she said a name. "Every one of those people was a friend, and now they're rotting in the ground."

"What? What are you talking about? It's a *game*." The Wurm's voice was uncertain. Norah turned on her radio magic. The first emotion that hit her was anger. After a moment, Norah realized that it wasn't coming from the Wurm. Nope, that crimson wash of fury was roaring out of her mother.

The Wurm was angry too, but he was more subdued. He was being detained unjustly. He was concerned for his equipment, and he desperately hoped they were lying to him.

"You didn't realize Dark Hound was real?" Norah asked. The Wurm oozed anxious fear and shook his head.

"I think he's telling the truth." She touched her mom's arm.

"What's your real name?" Petra asked.

The Wurm snorted. "Uriel. Uriel Chukwu."

"Okay, Uriel. Who paid you to do this?"

"Look, someone contacted one of my dark web profiles and asked me to put together some code. He said he wanted to play a game with his friends, but they were all hackers and didn't consider hacking to be cheating. So, it had to be rock solid. The Fort Knox of code. I did good work, but it wasn't fancy."

"It was fancy enough to kill people." Norah stared at a pulsing red starburst.

"You need to shut down the site," Andrew said.

Uriel shook his head. "I wrote the code. I don't run the site. It's all hosted on a server farm."

"Where's the farm?" Petra asked. Pepe stuck his tongue very near Uriel's eye to underscore her point.

"I don't know. Somewhere with a lot of cooling and a lot of power."

"Like your lair?" Norah asked.

"No. Bigger. Way bigger."

"Have you met your contact for the Dark Hound project? Maybe you can set up a meeting."

"We only used code names, and all our communication was encrypted. People on the dark web don't surf around, flashing their IDs for every facial recognition algorithm to track."

When the stick fails, try the carrot.

"You're supposed to be a genius hacker, right? Can you track this guy down?"

"Maybe," Uriel said. "If I get my gear back."

Norah nodded. "I think it's time for you and Quint to pay a visit to Hazel."

Quint's expression became enthusiastic but wary, as if he was being invited to test a beautifully crafted guillotine.

"Try not to piss off your ancient and powerful light elf MILF girlfriend!" Andrew called cheerfully.

Pepe backed away, looking disappointed. Norah pulled an unripe lemon off the nearest tree and tossed it to him like a tennis ball, which mollified him.

Andrew, who should have been mercilessly teasing Quint about Hazel, stared into the distance with a troubled look.

"What is it?" Norah asked.

There was a long pause, then, "Where the fuck did the Hollywood sign go?"

Norah kept expecting to get a call from the mayor, or the FBI, or Steven Spielberg, but her phone was alarmingly silent. According to the news, the Griffith Observatory was closed pending an investigation into possible magical tampering with its Tesla coil. The disappearance of the Hollywood sign was being treated as a simple act of vandalism. Still, she slept fitfully, dreaming about an enormous white O bawling for its supper.

Her eyes shot open. She'd heard a knock on the door. When she went to open it, an ErrandBoy in an orange t-shirt held out a white enamel box. "This is from Angelo Consoli," he said sullenly.

"What is it?" Norah asked, signing the kid's clipboard. He shrugged.

Before she opened the box, Norah unfolded the attached note.

Enjoy some canapés and my ongoing contrition. Sincerely, Angelo.

Inside was a large hinged case. When it was open, Norah blinked.

Angelo's gift was a dollhouse-sized kitchen with a tiny stove perched on a tiny oven next to a tiny sink. For kicks, Norah tried one of the taps. A minute stream of hot water shot out.

"Hello!" a cheerful voice exclaimed. Norah jumped.

A tiny wooden doll waved at her. Dressed in a white coat and a chef's toque, the four-inch figurine was perfectly scaled for the kitchen. His face seemed oddly familiar.

"Angelo?" Norah asked.

"Hello! I am Angelino," the figurine said. "Would you like a snack?"

"What is this?" Norah asked.

"Hello! Would you like a snack?" tiny Angelo repeated.

"Um, sure." Her affirmation produced a flurry of activity. She watched, fascinated, as the miniature chef opened the miniature refrigerator and removed a miniature chicken breast. It was like watching a TikTok of someone making tiny food for a hamster. She remained totally absorbed until the figurine presented her with a chicken sandwich the length of her thumb.

Norah ate it. Like everything Angelo made, assuming this counted, it was delicious. "It's very good."

"Thank you! Hello! Would you like a snack?"

Norah's phone beeped.

"Not now." She closed the kitchen's lid. She hoped that shut the tiny automaton down and did not force him to wait indefinitely in a dark box.

"I should introduce you to Cleo," she murmured and read the message. It was from the casting director of *Green & Pointy*.

Frondle's in.

CHAPTER FIVE

They celebrated at Musso and Frank. As she slid into a red leather banquette in the low lighting, Norah felt a flutter of excitement when Frondle's knee brushed hers under the table.

The restaurant was classic Old Hollywood, so classic that it had its own star on the Walk of Fame. With its white tablecloths and elderly waiters, it was old-fashioned. It was the perfect place to celebrate a deal.

"This is very kind of you."

"Oh, we're not celebrating *you*," Norah teased. "Getting a client a lead role on a sitcom is hitting the jackpot. You do all the work, and I cash those sweet, sweet checks."

"The pilot might not get picked up," Frondle pointed out.

He was right. The network hadn't ordered a season yet, but Norah had a good feeling about the project.

"A hundred episodes and a movie. I can smell it."

Frondle touched Norah's hand. "I appreciate everything you've done for me. Truly."

The charge between them rivaled the output of a runaway Tesla coil, and Frondle withdrew.

"Scorsese always gets the sand dabs. Should I get those?" Norah asked.

"What's a sand dab?" Frondle asked.

"I have no idea, but if it's good enough for Scorsese..."

Clementine, the server who took their drink order, seemed to have been air-dropped in from a Wisconsin beauty pageant. Norah ordered two martinis. Gin was great when you wanted to feel like your brains had been scooped out by a pine tree, which Norah did.

There was a noise over her shoulder and Norah turned, expecting to see her drink. Instead, it was Dakota, the casting assistant from Frondle's audition. "Hey, guys! Celebrating your big win?"

When she saw their hands clasped on the table, she froze. Then her face went pleasant again. Uneasily, Norah realized that Frondle was staring at her with open admiration. *Endearing, but this is not the time.*

Norah detached her hand from Frondle's and smiled.

"I'm having the sand dabs. Like Scorsese."

"I think it was Spielberg." Dakota had a hesitant look on her face. The server chose that moment to crowd their table with a tray of drinks. *Gin strikes again.*

"Don't drink too many of those," Dakota added, pointing at Frondle's martini. "They're deadly."

Frondle gave his martini a steely gaze and pulled a thread of light out of the flickering candle flame on the table, swirling it through his drink. The gin sparkled as if it had been dosed with mica. "It does not appear to be poisoned," he told Norah.

Amazement overtook Dakota's face. "He's the real deal, huh? You hang onto this one."

"I will."

"As a client, I mean," Dakota added. She excused herself but cast a measured glance over her shoulder.

When she left, Frondle leaned in. "Did I do something wrong?" The candlelight flickered invitingly off the flecks of gold around his pupils.

"Have you told people we're... Well, we're not doing anything. Except for that kiss."

Frondle slumped, looking bereft. Before he recited some tedious light elf poem about tarnished honor, Norah added, "Have you told people I'm more than your agent?"

"You mean that I am your oath-sworn companion in the destruction of Dark Hound?" Frondle asked.

"Hey, guys, do you know what you're having?" a chipper voice asked. Their server was back.

"Er..."

"The Dark Hound scoundrels will taste my blade," Frondle informed Clementine casually.

"Ooh, are you running lines? You know, I'm an actor, too."

"Norah's an agent." Only the glowing pride in his eyes prevented her from stabbing him with a butter knife.

"I'll have the sand dabs," Norah shot back before Clementine could slip her a headshot.

"Just like Scorsese!" Clementine cried.

They managed to finish their order without having to attend an impromptu monologue performance, and Norah swirled her olive, annoyed to be talking Dark Hound business. In short order, she caught Frondle up on recent developments.

"Uriel is trying to find out more about his contact. We're getting closer, I promise. I'm going to find that server farm."

"I am eager to redeem my word."

"Is that what the kids are calling it?" Norah muttered. Frondle looked confused, so she raised her martini glass. "To a hundred episodes of *Green & Pointy*."

"A hundred episodes," Frondle echoed.

Musso and Frank's kitchen was so hot that anyone who stopped moving risked becoming steamed meat. The edges of Clementine's blonde hair curled into a halo of frizz as she slipped a large pasta pot off a shelf and thudded out the back entrance. Finding a private space between two dumpsters, she plunked the shiny silver pot on the ground and brandished a small velvet bag. Pinching a fingerful of salt, she cast the grains on the mirror-polished aluminum. The light reflecting off the metal warped and swirled, and a dark silhouette appeared at the bottom of the pot.

"What?" a gravelly voice demanded.

"We have a problem." Clementine's chipper Midwestern twang had dissolved somewhere near the kitchen door. "That witch agent and her light elf boy toy are after Dark Hound."

The figure responded with an abyssal predatory growl. "Do you have any updates that aren't two months old and a complete waste of my fucking time?"

"They know about the server farm."

A long silence, or what counted in Hollywood for silence, which involved a lot of background helicopter blades and shouting.

"Stay on top of them," the voice said.

"Like hollandaise on sand dabs," Clementine proclaimed.

"That sounds fucking disgusting." Without warning, the reflection in the enormous pasta pot reverted to an image of Clementine's face. She blew a kiss to herself and slung the pot over her shoulder, then whistled her way back to the kitchen.

CHAPTER SIX

S ix carrots danced around an oversized mixing bowl like synchronized swimmers, their green tops waving as they pirouetted. Duncan stood behind this exuberant vegetal display, conducting the show with a wooden spoon that doubled as a wand.

"Carrots have a high sugar content," he stated cheerfully from beneath a massive chef's hat. His large head swam in the white fabric.

Veg with Reg was a new kid's show about nutrition and cooking, and Duncan had landed the lead role.

"I'm going to name my firstborn child after you." The young woman standing next to Norah in the wings sounded very serious.

"What if it's a boy?" Norah asked.

"I'll name him Norbert. I don't give a fuck. You are a lifesaver."

Without warning, Norah was enclosed in a bear hug.

Duncan, who had gotten famous on TikTok by doing funny magical stunts, had been trying to escape a hellacious Beverly Hills hype house full of shirtless twenty-something men who only came down from their keg stands to do molly.

After getting cast as the titular Reg, he'd been able to move into a normal apartment in a North Hollywood condo with his girlfriend Bea, who was halfway through law school. Her eyes were very clear and focused as she inspected the set for any whisper of trouble.

"I'm going to make him eat that cake when he's done with it. I did my time at the Palace, and I never want to see another abdominal muscle in my fucking life."

"Is his magic back to normal?"

"Basically. Sometimes I catch him chewing on his wand like he's trying to eat it, but nothing that would interfere with his work."

The *Veg with Reg* set was cute. The appliances had been sized up to make Duncan look like a kid in his parent's kitchen. As he stirred a large bowl of carrot cake batter, he bantered cheerfully with a character named Farmer Jenny.

"Cut!" the director called. "Let's reset for the cake pull. I want to push in with Camera Two."

The shoot had been frictionless so far, except that Angelo was running Craft Services. Duncan had told Norah he was doing some culinary consulting as well. So far, it was all above board.

Angelo approached her with a tray of tiny cups filled with some Cheeto-orange whip.

"Carrot pudding? There's a touch of sunfruit in there to brighten things up. How do you like Angelino? Is he working hard for you?"

"To be honest, he's unsettling, but I'm so addicted to his

tiny chicken parm that I've put up with it," Norah stated grudgingly. Now she was hungry for chicken parm, but she settled for one of Angelo's puddings.

The dessert was amazing, smooth and earthy with a bright finish. Norah found that her first cup paired perfectly with three more cups. Angelo beamed as he took a leaning stack of dishes back from her.

"I'm going to watch the cake pull," Norah stated, mouth half-full of orange pudding.

She found a good vantage point behind the cameras to watch the big moment when the carrot cake came out of the oven. The director called action, and an odd, high-pitched noise rang through the room. A light flickered overhead, and when Duncan opened the oven, a column of black smoke forced its way out.

"Cut!" the director called. "What the fuck is that?"

Duncan tried to shut the oven but struggled against the smoke. The plume was alive. After a moment, there was a thundering *pop*, and Duncan flew back against the kitchen island. Oversized spoons clattered onto the tiled floor.

The oven door clanked open, and Norah's eyes watered as the fingers of smoke became a roiling cloud. A cake floated from the oven, tipping out of its baking tin into the air. It split into two half-moons, revealing the jagged edges of almonds studded into the rounds like gnashing teeth.

Rather than dispersing, the smoke collected in a dense cloud around this cake mouth, making a shape like a rippling skull.

"Is that intentional?" Bea looked fearfully at Duncan's crumpled body.

Norah shook her head. "I don't think so." She pulled out

her wand and took a defensive stance as a PA ran over to the skull with a fire extinguisher.

With a deep, eerie laugh, the skull sucked the white foam into its mouth. It went gray, and it seemed rabid.

An operator holding a Steadicam tripped over a sandbag as he backed away from the apparition. Norah cringed as the camera smashed into the concrete floor.

The laugh subsided, and Norah relaxed fractionally. Then a deep voice replaced it.

"Give up, Norah Wintry!" the skull boomed, shedding almond teeth and crumbs as the cake mouth opened and closed. A lot of people in Los Angeles were terrified of cake, but this was beyond the pale.

"Give up, Norah Wintry!" the cake demanded again. It belched through its chasm of a mouth, exhaling glowing red wisps that swirled and condensed into three-dimensional images.

Norah gasped. Her parents' heads, glowing a transparent red, floated above the studio floor just as they appeared on Dark Hound.

Except now, red starbursts bloomed between their eyes.

"Give up or else!"

Norah, scrambling to respond, shot a stunning spell at the smoky skull, but the blue stream of magic passed through the mist without disturbing it.

When she was about to throw a magical net over it, the skull collapsed, dropped out of the air, and disintegrated against the concrete. The smoke diffused into a formless haze.

Bea rushed to Duncan. Norah scrambled to her feet and

found the couple staring at her. A small cut on Duncan's temple bled profusely, and she raised her wand to heal it.

"Don't," Duncan said. "I think you should go."

"Duncan?" Norah asked. He shook his head.

"Norah, you have no idea how grateful I am for this job. If I'd stayed in the Palace for one more day, someone would have teabagged me to death. Now Bea and I are in a good place, and I can't afford any screwups. I don't think you should come to the set anymore. Can't you, like, send emails?"

The air around her feet had become molasses. Everything moved in slow motion. Had the lights dimmed?

"Please." The desperation in Duncan's voice spurred her to action.

"Sure. I can send emails," Norah said. "But I want you to know that the person who did this won't be at it long. I'm going to get them."

As she left the studio, she kept an eye out for Angelo.

Like the skull, he had disappeared into thin air.

CHAPTER SEVEN

Norah poured half a bottle of Floe down her throat, the tasteless liquid splashing through her parched lips.

"You know that's a real Floe, not one of the tap refills," Madge gruffly informed her from her perch on Norah's monitor.

Light danced off the sleek glass bottle. "Add me to the list of people who can't tell the difference," Norah stated. Aspirin and healing magic hadn't made a dent in her headache, so maybe ten dollars' worth of water would.

A thunderous bang sent the pain in Norah's temple rattling around her skull as the office door opened. Instead of swinging in on its hinges, it splintered and fell inward, thudding against the floor.

A Kilomea stepped gingerly into the gap with a sheepish expression on her face.

Most Kilomeas wore practical clothing like leathers and tunics if they weren't in full armor. This one wore a taffeta party dress printed with tiny hearts. More distressingly, she had bedazzled her curving horns with pink rhinestones. Staring from the broken door to the party dress, Norah wondered if she was under some kind of romantic attack.

"Oh, my God! I'm so sorry about your door! I was soooo excited about this meeting. My adrenaline's been pumping since about six this morning, and my therapist says I should be more assertive, so I wanted to knock assertively. But then, she's a pixie. She could probably kick someone in the eyeball without them noticing since she's so tiny. She doesn't understand the risks of being assertive when you're a Kilomea in a human world."

She pried the door off the floor and attempted to set it back in place. Several shiny pieces of shattered hinge lay on the carpet, so it was a losing battle. Madge sat on the edge of Norah's bookshelf, pulled a piece of popcorn from a nearby bowl, and settled in to watch...whatever this was.

"You're, uh, Sweetie?" Norah asked, glancing at her calendar.

The Kilomea abandoned her repair efforts and leaned the door against the wall, then spun and stuck her hand out for Norah to shake.

"Sweetie Sandobal."

A piece of shattered brass glinted on the floor, so Norah shook the offered hand with extreme hesitation, hoping Sweetie's exuberance did not extend to bone-crushing.

The grip was painful but caused no permanent damage. Norah rubbed her fingers and attempted a smile as the Kilomea chattered on.

"I was so excited that you wanted to meet me. I'm not anyone important, just a little Kilomea from out in the hinterlands. You represent such amazing people. I absolutely love the Dunker. I watch him on TikTok all the time."

Before this flood of words carried Norah into the next century, she cut Sweetie off. "What are your professional goals?" This was an amazingly effective technique for separating people with achievable ambitions from people with a vague lust for fame.

"I want to write Hallmark Christmas movies, and after I've written ten or fifteen, I want to direct them," Sweetie announced, running a nervous hand over a horn. Pink rhinestones rained onto Norah's carpet, and Sweetie, biting a long talon, apologized again and bent down to collect them.

"Don't worry about that." Norah loved having a specific goal, especially a weird, unpretentious one. The mere mention of Hallmark movies put a mean smirk on most faces in Hollywood. There was, she admitted, a factory-like quality to them, but the great thing about factories was that they needed factory workers.

"Those kinds of movies aren't, uh, very lucrative."

Sweetie's smile failed to dim. "They are if you write ten a year." She reached for her purse, which was a large pink suitcase, pulled out a tower of paper, and plunked it on the desk. "This is what I wrote last year."

Ten scripts sat in the pile. Norah glanced at the title on the first one. *"The Best is Yeti to Come."*

"It's about a Kilomea from the big city who goes to a struggling ski resort to relax over Christmas, but she gets mistaken for a yeti, which attracts tourists, so she and the handsome ski resort owner have to keep their relationship a secret, so he doesn't go bankrupt."

Norah downed more of the Floe and thought about it. "I'd watch that." Sweetie beamed as the rep thumbed through the scripts, which included potential hits like *I'll Be Gnome for Christmas* and *The Elf and the Elves.*

"Are they all about magicals?" Norah asked.

Sweetie shook her head. "There are two conventional ones in there as samples. To be honest, they're my worst work. Oh! I have a gift for you!"

Sweetie reached inside the pink suitcase and produced a garish snow globe. Inside was a reproduction of her head wearing a Santa hat. She shook the globe so vigorously before dropping it on the desk that it almost broke.

Shoes scuffed on the carpet, and a head peeked warily into the space left by the broken door. It was Castor, and he had his wand out. "Is everything okay in here?"

On Norah's desk, glittering snow fell on miniature horns. The globe was so ridiculous that she felt great affection for it.

Castor gazed warily at the eyeball-burning heart print on Sweetie's dress. "Should I come back later?"

"It'll take a while to get through this stack." Norah put her hand protectively on the stack of scripts. The Kilomea slumped. "But I promise, I'm intrigued. I am. Let's meet back up in a week or so?"

Madge buzzed. "I love Christmas movies. Have you had lunch? The place downstairs does an incredible pizza," she chattered as she walked the Kilomea out.

Castor sat in the chair across from Norah's desk and fidgeted until she demanded that he spill the beans.

"I should have called."

"What is it?"

"Lottie won't meet you."

Norah grimaced. "Why not?"

Castor put his hands on his hips. "Because she's a mean old lady who's set in her ways and doesn't care about other people?"

That might be true. On the other hand, Castor wasn't the world's most likable petitioner.

"Where does she live?" Norah asked. "Convincing mean people to do things they don't want to do is seventy percent of my job as an agent."

"It's far away."

Norah crossed her arms and stared at Castor until he wrote down an address.

On the drive to Big Bear, Madge entertained them with a story about a squirrel that had been dropping nuts on her roof for weeks.

"I'm either going to serve him for dinner or tame him and ride him around my neighborhood," the pixie concluded. Madge would look good riding a squirrel.

Hazel chuckled and looked out the window as the urban sprawl mellowed into a pine forest scattered with country homes.

"I love the woods." The fire elemental had a hungry look in her eyes. "So much fuel."

Inviting a fire elemental to the forest was a bold decision, but Norah had a gut feeling that Hazel would be useful. They'd only spoken for a minute when Norah had dropped off Uriel's computer equipment.

"Seriously, I haven't been to Big Bear in years. No one ever invites me on their ski trips. They claim I melt their powder."

Using fire to encourage a puppeteer's cooperation was a grimy trick, but Cleo was worth it. Following the map on her phone, Norah pulled off Highway 330 and headed into the San Bernardino mountains on a gravel road. The road rattled the chassis, and twice Norah's head hit the ceiling. After a few minutes of being thrown around the car, Norah wished she'd worn a sports bra. Once or twice, she thought she noticed movement in the trees, but the twisting road quickly reclaimed her attention.

When she was sure she couldn't go any farther, a metallic thud rang out, and her car stopped dead.

"Did we hit something?" Norah asked. After a moment of silence, the car shifted, and something hard scraped across the ceiling.

"I don't think we hit anything," Madge whispered, hovering above the passenger's seat. "I think something hit us."

Another bang, and something scratched on the metal. A shadow fell across the windshield, and Madge dropped onto the seat in surprise as an enormous shining dragon dented the hood.

It wasn't a real dragon, or not an organic one. As long as a mature boa constrictor, it was carved from individual wooden segments united by clever joints. What seemed to be swirls of paint were wood grain, an Oriceran tree with alternating black-and-white rings twisting in complicated patterns like the folds of a brain. Scale-like sequins crusted the construct's back, and its eyes were made of blown glass. It was twelve feet long, and the sinuous wood wound through the air with no regard for the constraints of gravity. The ribbon of a body twisted as its small legs clung to rocks and branches.

Norah scrambled out of the car, wand pointed. The dragon spiraled into the road, coiling like a snake to block her path. The jaws opened, revealing white-enameled metal teeth that were silver at their razor-sharp tips.

"Go away," it hissed, its voice hollow. The front half of the dragon's body reared, and it shot like a jack-in-the-box over the hood of the car onto a branch ten feet above Norah's shoulder. The dragon seemed disinterested in the shield she raised, and its back legs clamped down on her front bumper. The dragon accordioned in on itself, and the car moved with a metallic creak.

Shit. I paid that car off.

Norah shot a blade of blue magic toward the dragon, but it moved faster than the spell, spinning her car and then releasing the bumper, which detached. The front wheels touched down with a thud, and Hazel shrieked from the back seat.

"Go away," the dragon repeated and leapt back into the tree. It had spun the car to point it back toward where they'd come from. That was an unambiguous message.

Norah dove back into the driver's seat and stuck her keys in the ignition.

Hazel leaned in from the back seat. "Can you create a spherical shield?"

Norah nodded.

"Can you create two?" Hazel continued.

"I think so."

"Great. Get one around the monster and follow my lead."

With that, Hazel jumped out of the car.

The dragon responded with a roar that blew leaves off the nearby trees. As Norah scrambled into the whipping wind, Hazel's eyes blazed, and she raised her hands. Small balls of fire budded above the pads of her fingers, and her brown skin flickered orange as she shot the balls one by one at the dragon. They bobbed toward the sequined scales and polished wood, and the dragon dodged effortlessly, its black-and-white jaws curling in a sneer.

Hazel loosed the fireballs from her left hand, floating them in a lazy agglomeration.

What was she doing? The dragon coiled as fireballs floated around it, and Norah realized what was happening.

Hazel was herding it. The dragon, flanked in three dimensions, twisted in on itself, coiling tighter and tighter. Hazel screamed, "Now!"

Norah's wand spilled a sheet of blue light that wafted around the dragon and closed in. The dragon clawed at the sheen of magic and raked a long line through it, but Hazel had it surrounded by fire. By clawing through the shield, the dragon exposed itself to licking flames. The construct screeched and curled tighter.

"Throw the second one around the first." Hazel filled the air with glowing fire. Norah closed the first shield and began a second one. As it curved around the first, Hazel filled the space between the shields with fire. It was like a fire bonbon if the nougat wanted to kill you.

As Norah closed the second sphere, Hazel surveyed the forest. A small bush burned at the edge of the road, and she sucked the flames toward her and absorbed them.

It was neat work. The dragon couldn't escape without being burned, and the forest was safe from immolation. However, the crackling orange orb wouldn't last forever.

"Should we keep going?" Hazel asked.

Norah shook her head and pointed at the trapped dragon, which was an angry spool of twisted wood and enamel inside its fiery cage.

"I don't think so. Did you notice that the dragon's leg has been repaired? It looks like it broke in half, but someone glued it together, sanded it, and repainted it. There are repair lines in the teeth, too, and lots of the sequins have been reglued. Plus, it's been treated with some kind of expensive-smelling oil."

"So what?" Hazel asked.

"So, Lottie loves this dragon. I'll bet you a thousand bucks she comes to save it."

Hazel didn't have time to take Norah up on her offer because the sound of wood on rock rose from the road in the distance.

Cartwheels? No, something more mechanical.

A shape the size of a VW bus raced toward them. Constructed from wood, the thing was a cross between a jaguar and a spider. Its six articulated wooden legs, meticulously painted with rune-saturated jaguar spots, carried a raised platform. The thing had a feline face on a long neck that undulated through the trees, swinging back and forth to survey its surroundings. A platform lined with an emerald-green velvet cushion sat upon the creature's back. The creature's movements were so fluid that the platform barely bobbed as its spidery legs skittered through the forest.

The witch riding the cushion was old and shrunken but spry enough to sit cross-legged. Spry enough, also, to carry and aim a rifle almost as tall as she was.

"Nobody move," the old witch called, and the jaguar head darted out and roared to underscore her orders. "My aim would be impeccable if my eyesight wasn't shit, but unfortunately for you, I'm what my ophthalmologist calls an 'uncorrectable.' I default to spraying bullets far and wide and for a considerable duration."

"We're here to talk. My friend needs your help."

"Oh, yeah? Does your friend need an octogenarian to complain about the weather and tell her that her work is shit?"

"No."

"Then sorry," the witch said. "Too bad. Boohoo. Those are my main skill sets. Now, you can either release my dragon, or you can bleed out in the underbrush and be an afternoon snack for the fat black bear who lives around these parts. I call him Badger, and aside from my wooden companions, he's the only creature in a four-thousand-mile radius I have any affection for."

"Why would you name a bear 'Badger?'" Hazel asked.

"Because calling him Bear seemed reductive. Now. Release. My. Dragon."

Lottie waved the rifle barrel in an anxiety-inducing swoosh that covered most of Norah's favorite vital organs.

"My friend is made of wood," Norah informed her. "She's a cursed box."

"That's what I said about my ex-wife," Lottie retorted.

Hazel snorted appreciatively.

"Unless you agree to talk to us, I'll release the shield between your friend and it will become basilisk brûlée."

Lottie hissed, a noise almost identical to the dragon's voice. Birds of a feather, apparently. "You wouldn't dare."

Norah tightened her grip on her wand, wondering how many bullets she could remove with what was left of her magical reserves.

After a moment, the woman's small body crumpled in on itself, and she dropped the rifle on the cushion beside her.

"Fine. I need some tea anyway. If you can keep up with Clarence, we will talk."

CHAPTER EIGHT

Norah could never remember what poison oak looked like, and the mad dash through the underbrush left her with no time to google it. Madge huffed above as she hurdled logs and crashed through lattices of branches, trying to keep up with the monstrous device. For the first time, she missed her flying shoes. Hazel had overtaken Norah and was loping through the forest with no apparent effort, long limbs always seeming to find the right foothold.

Lottie's spider-thing had stayed on the road for only a minute before veering into the trees. Norah thought the old witch was trying to lose them, but she maintained a pace it was barely possible to match. The dragon soared above the trees, casting snaky shadows on the underbrush and raising the hair on the back of Norah's neck. She half-expected to feel its enamel teeth bite into her.

Norah was drenched in sweat and probably poison oak when they reached a wooden cabin. It had a small footprint but soared three stories into the sky. The steep roof stretched over a small porch, where a single wicker rocking chair swayed. A gutter along the edge of the roof fed a large plastic rain barrel, whose contents were piped into the house.

These details were hard to appreciate since Norah's eyes were drawn to the chicken legs that held the house aloft. Eight feet tall, with mechanical joints at the knees and ankles, they were carved from the same black-and-white wood as the dragon and the jaguar-spider. They remained at their full height until Lottie cried, "Down, girl!"

The house squatted, and a short ramp unfurled from the doorway like a lolling tongue. The jaguar-spider flattened on the ground. Lottie hauled herself off the velvet cushions with conspicuous creaks. The old witch inspected the joints of her steed as it clambered back up, then patted one of its legs.

"Why don't you go find us a rabbit for supper?" she whispered. The construction shook with enthusiasm and dashed into the trees, its head swinging back and forth like a flashlight.

"I'm a vegetarian," Hazel stated.

Lottie glared. "Lucky for you, you're not invited."

The house shivered as they traipsed up the ramp. The interior shone with hardwood and hand-carved furniture. Lottie clearly didn't get much company. There was a single chair at the small kitchen table, and Lottie collapsed onto it with crossed arms.

"Stand or find a place on the floor." She waved a hand. Hazel stood. Norah, dripping with sweat, dropped onto the first step of the wooden staircase in the corner of the room. There was a wood stove for heating, a small range powered by a propane tank, and a sink.

"So, if you live in an, um, extremely mobile home, what's at the end of that road?" Norah asked.

"A big red herring," Lottie said. "No one ever makes it that far."

Lottie got up and made tea on the range, selecting herbs from a series of clear glass jars hanging in the window. She didn't offer Norah or Hazel a cup.

When Lottie was again ensconced in her chair, she sipped her tea and nodded. "Tell me about your wooden friend."

Norah described Cleo's problem and the curse that had transformed her into a wooden crate, the flying shoes that had given her new mobility, and Castor's efforts to make her functional hands.

"That grubby little shitkicker has an eye for carving," Lottie muttered, which Norah was sure was a glowing compliment.

When she was finished, Lottie shook her head. "I have a special affinity for living wood, but I can't help your friend. Making a construct with real life to it requires brainwood."

"Is that what your constructs are made out of?" Norah asked. Outside, the black-and-white-whorled dragon was preening.

Lottie nodded. "You can only get it in Oriceran, and only if you're willing to cut down hordes of irate wood elves."

"Did you do that?" Norah asked, hand on her wand.

"No." An apologetic expression flickered across Lottie's face. "My old man did and left me the wood in his will. I sold off a piece to buy this land, but the rest I kept for personal use. I am essentially living in my inheritance."

"We don't need much."

"You need more than zero, which is how much I have."

Hazel stared at the preening dragon. Its middle section was folded into a tight serpentine. "Your dragon's awfully long. What if we took a segment from its middle?"

Lottie's eyes blazed with as much fire as Norah had ever seen from Hazel. "What a tremendous idea," she spat.

"Really?" Hazel asked.

Norah could tell by the way Lottie's face scrunched that she'd made a huge mistake.

"Sure," Lottie said. "Let's go ahead and chop one of my only friends in this world in half and rip out his stomach. I'm sure he'll be fine."

"You can't reconstruct him?" Norah asked.

"Not without changing him. The wood has a life of its own. That dragon's been up and about for thirty years, and I'm sure that by this point, he's conscious. I'm not putting him under the knife."

Hazel snorted. "It's a bunch of animated parts."

Lottie's head swiveled with great precision. "*You're* a bunch of animated parts. How about I take a few of your vertebrae? You have so many."

Hazel crossed her arms protectively over her stomach.

"That's what I thought." Lottie sneered. "Pfft. Little Miss Vegetarian. I don't care what you're made of. Conscious is conscious."

The blinking eyes of the Hollywood sign drifted into Norah's mind. *Shit.*

"If you can get your hands on some brainwood, I'll

teach Mr. Hotshit Boogerpicker what I know about carving it."

"Really?" Norah asked.

"Sure, why not? You'll never find the wood, so it's no skin off my back. Now, if you would be so kind as to fuck off, I'll have Clarence take you back to your car."

Norah scratched a red rash rising on her ankle and grudgingly clambered to her feet.

The drive back to LA was long and quiet. When she pulled into her apartment complex, she didn't bother to drop off her stuff. Instead, she made a beeline for Stan's door. After a full minute of pounding went unanswered, she tried calling him. Nothing.

When Norah was starting to worry, Billy Warble, her wizard neighbor, came out from next door. "Stan didn't tell you? He's on vacation."

"Really?"

"It was a last-minute trip. He and Minnie went to Antarctica."

"Isn't it winter there? Who goes to Antarctica in the winter?"

"Vampires. There's a zippy tourism industry there for our fanged friends. I wouldn't be caught dead in subzero temperatures, but I guess twenty-four hours of darkness a day is heaven for the vamps. I think McMurdo is having a death metal music festival."

Norah swore under her breath. It was not that Stan didn't deserve a vacation. He had just picked a shitty time. If anyone understood wood, it was him.

Madge buzzed over and perched on the leaves of a hanging jade plant, then swung from it cheerfully. After a particularly vigorous swing, the stem snapped, tossing Madge into a nearby aloe plant. She swore and poked at a hole in her jumpsuit. "Do you need to be reminded that you *know* an Oriceran importer? One who can get almost anything?"

Norah's stomach dropped. She was willing to risk eating a piece of perma-sushi every so often, but importing rare and dubiously ethical wood?

"I still don't trust Angelo. Not enough for this, anyway. Look what happened on set the other day. He may have been involved."

"Having an evil dad doesn't make *him* evil. It makes him owe you a favor. Several favors, in fact."

"No. Not yet. Cleo's too important."

When she finally made it into her apartment, she took the lid off the tiny kitchen Angelo had sent her and stared at the small figure, wondering if the caterer was really her only option.

CHAPTER NINE

"Is it weird that you're here?" Frondle asked. "Mal's agent isn't."

"The range of behavior considered normal from actors is as vast and continuously expanding as the universe. You're fine." Norah was trying to convince herself as much as him. Her client list was in good shape, and she might have come even if she wasn't desperate to spend time with him. Frondle's face glowed in the reflection from the hair and makeup mirror. The stylist was trimming the blond hair around his ears to show them off. You couldn't have a show called *Green & Pointy* without some points.

Frondle, script in hand, murmured lines.

The makeup artist, a chunky no-nonsense blonde named Dallas, loitered in a folding chair, waiting for her turn. She stared at Frondle, enraptured. "His skin is so perfect. It looks like porcelain. Really expensive porcelain."

"And it feels like velvet."

The makeup woman raised an eyebrow. "Are you two..."

"No!" Norah panicked. "I mean, whenever I shake his hand or pat him on the back."

Pat him on the back? What are you, his rugby coach?

"So, in this back-patting scenario, he's not wearing a shirt?" Dallas asked.

A bead of sweat rolled down Norah's forehead. "I'm going to get Frondle a healthy snack," she announced and fled the conversation. While he finished hair and makeup, she sequestered herself in a corner and stared at her phone screen until her eyes burned.

"We're gonna shoot the bar scene first," the director shouted. The white-haired man, whose name was Benji, looked old enough to have mentored the Lumière Brothers. Frondle shook hands with Mal. The bottle-green crystal person had been painstakingly polished and sported a few new facets on his head. Apparently, he'd been scouted for the show on Oriceran.

"Places!" Benji shouted. Frondle sat at the bar, and Mal joined him.

"You two are bonding," Benji said. "Show me the bond. Action!"

Mal slipped effortlessly into character. "I've been struggling to pay the rent since Topaz moved out. Last month, I had to break off a toe to cover it."

"What happened between you two?" Frondle asked, face open and vulnerable.

Mal smirked. "She wanted a diamond." He paused to sip the prop beer in front of him. "I didn't realize she meant my brother."

Benji nodded and glanced at his script. "Laugh, laugh,

laugh, very nice. One more for safety, then we're moving on."

When the bar scene was done, they moved across the studio to do a scene at a Brooklyn psychic's shop. Mal kept trying to eat the psychic's crystals while she wasn't looking. He was much funnier than Frondle, who had only been given a few scattered laugh lines.

Some of Frondle's jokes from the original script had been given to Mal. As Norah watched the big crystal person land laugh after laugh, she became disturbed and went to find the showrunner.

Ursula was a hard-bitten middle-aged woman whose Botox made her look perpetually happy. This was misleading, as one discovered after five minutes with her. She barely glanced up from her laptop when Norah approached.

"It's you. Frondle's dedicated, ah, *agent*." Ursula gave the last word a sardonic twist.

Norah ignored the jab. "Where did Frondle's jokes go?"

Ursula shrugged. "Every show needs a straight man."

"Any straighter, and you could use him as a level."

"His comic timing has a ways to go. He still gets that bodega scene. It's very funny when he eats that magazine."

"Look, I want to be sure Bernard feels confident in the show's full range of talent when they watch the pilot."

Bernard was the chief creative executive at the network. He primarily bought comedies, though Norah had never seen him smile. The man was shaped like a stick of gray chalk.

"We can go back to the original script for the tour of the apartment. How about that?"

"Great. Thanks, Ursula."

When she went back to watch the shoot, they were filming the tag.

"I'm all ears!" Frondle cried.

"Let's take that again," Benji ordered. "I want more enthusiasm. Really hammer me with your painful optimism."

The camera reset, and they ran the scene again. At the end, Frondle said, "I'm all ears!" Norah cringed. He'd done it the same way the second time.

The director, she could tell, was starting to lose interest in him.

"Let's take five," the director stated. Frondle, tracking Benji's discontent, trotted over to Norah.

"Am I doing an okay job?" he asked, voice quavering.

He needed tough love. She could feel it in her bones. Honesty was a dangerous tool to use with an actor, but sometimes it was essential.

She couldn't bring herself to do it. If she told him he was blowing it, he would look sad. He was already down about his honor.

"You're doing awesome. You're a comedy superstar, Frondle. Everyone's going to love it."

His face brightened, and Norah's stomach lining worried at a pearl of anxiety. The shoot was going fine. At least no one had threatened her with reanimated cake.

Norah ducked out of the shoot early like a coward and texted Frondle a few anodyne congratulations when she got home. Sighing, she collapsed onto the couch and pulled a script off the smoky glass coffin she continued to use as a coffee table. "Want to help me with my coverage?" she asked Garton Saxon's frozen face.

She spent a good chunk of the next few days reading Sweetie's scripts. When her brain folds were thoroughly flossed with tinsel, she googled everyone who worked for Hallmark until she found a producer she'd worked with as a PA with on a memorably bad set five years ago. Suni had worn leggings on the first day of the shoot, and the director had called her "Hotpants" for three weeks. Norah had been "the Stick," apparently a reference to both her wand and the fact that she didn't smile enough.

"Hey, Suni. It's Norah," she said when the call went through.

"Who?" Suni asked.

"Um, the Stick from *Double Barrel Trouble*."

"Oh, my God, Stick! How many years has it been?"

"Not enough to repair the trauma."

"I haven't worn leggings since. But I'm sure you didn't call to relive the bad old days."

"Hah. I have an interesting new writer in my pocket. Does Hallmark have a mandate for magical romances? Er, that is, romances starring magicals?"

There was typing on the other end of the line.

"We're making one this year. It's called *We Wish You a Fairy Christmas*."

"So, it's about gnomes," Norah joked. The pause was followed by a forced tinkle of laughter.

Norah cleared her throat. "I'm going to send over a couple of scripts. I have this new writer. She's kind of Christmas-obsessed and is churning out fun work. My personal favorite is *I'll be Gnome for Christmas*, which is about a gnome working at a mall who falls in love with one of the elves. *Christmas* elves, not elf-elves. Anyway, I'm emailing you now."

There was a faint ding on the other end of the line. Suni's cheerful voice came back on. "It's in my inbox. I'll take a look!"

"Thanks. Talk to you later, Hotpants."

Norah hung up, pulled open her desk drawer, and popped open her container of perma-sushi, then inhaled some unagi. *Curse you, Angelo.* The fish was delicious. Plenty of people would forgive significantly greater crimes for sushi that good.

Stay strong, Wintry. As she shut the lid of the box, her phone beeped.

The network executives were ready to watch a cut of Frondle's pilot. Norah put it in her calendar and set three alerts.

CHAPTER TEN

Three days later, she picked Frondle up for the screening. It was a coin toss as to who was more nervous. Frondle tapped his fingers on his knee as they drove.

"Once, during my years in the Light Elf Solar Vanguard, my unit was set upon by feral unicorns. They killed my captain and punched a hole in the armor I'd spent six years saving up for."

"Oh, my God."

Frondle shivered. "This is worse."

Norah patted his hand. "Okay, don't freak out if they don't laugh at the jokes. Television executives are more like money-sniffing robots than human beings."

"What if they hate it?" Frondle asked.

"Then I will get you another pilot audition, and another, and another until I die of old age while you continue your career as Hollywood's permanent ingénue."

Norah put her hand on Frondle's thigh, and he met her gaze.

"How could anyone fail to love you?" she asked.

They spent a long minute staring at each other, then Norah cleared her throat. "Once more into the breach."

The auditorium was ugly and poorly lit, with taupe walls and surplus brown carpet. The show would have to dazzle more than the décor. Norah politely waved at a few people and took an unobtrusive seat in the corner. She considered saying hello to Bernard, but the executive was surrounded by an impenetrable barrier of aides and direct-reports. The emotional climate was subdued.

Frondle stayed on his feet and paced the aisle.

Benji was confabbing with Mal in the corner, and each time Frondle reached the end of his aisle, he took two steps toward them, then veered away. It hurt to watch.

Norah was relieved when he rejoined her.

"It's going to be okay," She weighed the wisdom of hugging him but settled for a warm smile. "One time, an executive fell asleep during a screening of a client's show. Slept through the whole second act."

"And the show got canceled?" Frondle asked.

"The network bought twelve episodes. You never know."

After a few more minutes of watching various executives, including Bernard, effortlessly join Mal and Benji's circle, Norah's eye twitched. She tapped the arm of her chair with a fingernail until the lights finally dimmed and the opening notes of the *Green & Pointy* theme song jingled into the room, playing over establishing shots of Italian bistros and the WNYC Transmitter Park.

Frondle and Mal popped onto the screen, strolling

along a street in Greenpoint until Frondle tripped into an open sidewalk cellar door.

No one laughed. Not one snicker. Norah wanted to whisper something comforting to Frondle, but it was so quiet that it would have been like shouting into a megaphone.

Norah had thought she understood silence. Over the course of the screening, she realized she had only begun to plumb its depths. It was like watching TV in a mausoleum. There was the sound from the episode, so people's breathing was not audible above the laugh track and music stings. But each joke, when delivered, seemed to generate a dense pool of noiselessness in the room. The juxtaposition of the laugh track further concentrated the ball of dead air. Frondle squirmed like a toddler until Norah elbowed him in the side.

Even worse, the show was funny. Norah would have bet money on it. However, the atmosphere oppressed her will to laugh, and it set in on her will to live. Thankfully, network television episodes were only twenty-two minutes long. She sank so far into her seat that it melded with her body. Watching a career-defining sitcom with network executives must have been an experience invented by the Spanish Inquisition to deal with particularly recalcitrant prisoners.

The audience clapped at a volume pitched above politeness, and the lights went back up.

Bernard stood and fiddled with his Rolex. "Good work. Very funny. Let's talk in my office, Ursula." He said it like he was inviting her to watch an execution.

As the showrunner walked past her, Norah resisted an

urge to ask if she had any final messages for her loved ones. She didn't meet Frondle's eyes.

"What do we do now?" Frondle asked.

"Have you ever had a Best Fish Taco?"

"Is that an American sex euphemism?"

"No! Well, sort of, but I'm talking about actual tacos. Lunch."

"Oh. I meant, what do we do about the show?" Frondle whispered.

Norah sighed. "We have to wait. Look, these fish tacos are great, and they're like two bucks. Perfect for an unemployed actor."

Frondle's face collapsed before the words were out of her mouth. "Can I come back to your place?"

Norah's breath caught in her throat, and she glanced around to see if anyone was listening. "Are you sure?"

Frondle nodded gravely. "I am going to stand over the Wurm's shoulder with a naked blade until his search for the Dark Houndmaster produces results."

Ah. Norah got to her feet. "Uriel's living on the roof of First Arret. I'll take you there, but I'm getting fish tacos first."

CHAPTER ELEVEN

The sensation that she was being watched increased as Norah picked up her pace on the trail in Western Canyon. She'd avoided Griffith Park since the fight at the observatory, but the run through her neighborhood was getting boring, so she'd decided to bite the bullet. Gravel crunched under her rhythmic footfalls, and the hair on the back of her neck prickled.

She glanced over her shoulder, but the only thing on the trail behind her was a twenty-something yelling at her off-leash dog. The young woman, whose puffball of a miniature Pomeranian appeared to be named "Tarantino," screamed at a rustling bush three times in a row before her voice died in her throat. Norah followed the woman's eyeline up and almost screamed herself.

A white forty-five-foot-tall letter H straddled the trail in a colossal arch. Norah stared at it for three seconds before spinning on one foot and sprinting downhill as fast as her quadriceps would take her. Her measly human legs were no match for the Hollywood sign's stems, however, and the H cut her off. As she skidded to a stop on the gravel, an O rolled down the hillside toward her, followed by the remaining letters.

A week earlier, TMZ claimed to have seen two letters of the sign splashing in George Clooney's pool. They didn't have photos, though, and she hadn't wanted to believe it.

"What do you want?" Norah asked, hoping the answer wasn't, say, witch terrine.

The rest of the Hollywood sign caught up, the detached pieces moving in concert like a line of ants. The double Os blinked at her, eyes wide. "Mama?"

"You've got this all wrong. Okay, yes, I funneled a huge amount of electricity into a spell to make you a tiny bit sentient, but that doesn't mean I'm your mother."

The Os blinked again, clear liquid welling in the saddles. *Did I make the Hollywood sign cry?*

"Shoo!" Norah immediately felt guilty. She had clients to help and an evil webmaster to take down. She didn't have time to burp four stories of plywood, or whatever nurturing signage would entail. "Go on! Get out of here!"

Pulling out her wand, she lifted a small pebble and, after twirling it in a lazy circle, flung it at the sign. The pebble bounced harmlessly off the wood, but there was an enormous whine of metal, and one of the H's wide legs moved back, toppling a yucca.

"Go away!" Norah screamed. Like a weird caterpillar, the sign ran.

"Wow! You're so brave!" the young woman on the trail cried. Tarantino the Pomeranian, clutched in the woman's arms, narrowed its eyes, and loosed a threatening growl. "Why did it call you 'Mama?'"

"Uh…"

The ringtone on her phone freed her from the interaction. Norah excused herself with a wave of her fingers and put on her headset as she watched the sign retreat over the hill. It was Duncan.

"Duncan! The Dunker! How's it going? Is everything okay with *Veg with Reg?*"

"What? Oh, yeah, it's good. We shot celery today. I'm still pulling fiber out of my teeth."

"Is it balancing with the TikTok partnerships? Are you keeping it family-friendly?"

Duncan sounded uneasy. "Yeah, yeah, yeah. I actually called about the cake."

"The evil one?" Norah asked, stomach sinking.

"Yeah. I took a piece to a buddy of mine."

"To eat?" Norah asked, horrified.

"What? No! To analyze. He's a grad student at UCLA, working on hybrid magichemistry. He did a few tests and said it was made with impfruit."

"What is that?" Norah asked.

"I guess it makes food evil? I don't understand how it works. The dark elves use it for an anti-harvest festival."

"A Thanklessgiving."

"Anyway, I did some googling, and I found only one use of impfruit. Johnny Knoxville used it on a *Jackass* Easter reunion special a few years ago."

"Okay."

"You know who the caterer was on that shoot?"

Norah could guess. "Was it Angelo?"

"Yeah," Duncan agreed.

Over the past week, she'd eaten enough perma-sushi to deplete a small aquarium. Nausea crept into her throat.

———

The route back to Norah's car was downhill, and she took it at a run. Her angry sprint blended seamlessly into an angry drive, and she made it to Angelo's catering headquarters in record time. His commercial kitchen was located within a bland expanse of Burbank cubes. Norah pushed her way through thronging chefs, ignoring irritated shouts as white-coated people balancing steaming tureens dodged her.

Angelo was tasting soup when she found him, and she knocked the spoon out of his mouth. Red bisque splattered on the coat of a nervous young woman standing beside him, and Norah pushed between them.

"Evil cake!" she shouted, poking him in the chest.

Angelo frowned. "If one of my pastries has disappointed, I will cut out my heart with a cake server."

"Would that be sharp enough for major butchery?" the soup-splashed woman interjected.

Angelo fixed Norah with an intense gaze. "It is if you are very strong."

"Is that a threat?" Norah asked.

"It's a statement of confidence." Angelo's white coat moved as he flexed beneath his clothes.

Norah squared up. "If you want to mess with me and my work, fine, but you threatened my parents."

As she reached into her pocket, the soup chef shouted, "Wand!" Before Norah could get hers in the air, the business ends of eight wooden spoons were pointed at her heart, plus one hesitantly wielded bread knife.

Of course the man who stocked his kitchen with magical produce would hire magical chefs. "You're all wizards and witches," Norah stated.

"Not all of us!" the young man brandishing the bread knife, who was barely out of his teens, squeaked out.

Angelo rolled his eyes. "Stand down, Humphrey."

The bread knife dropped back toward a fresh-baked loaf of sourdough.

Norah took a deep breath and activated her radio magic. The emotions of the magical chefs reflected the tense atmosphere, but she sensed that their wand-spoons had been raised in defense, not offense. Angelo was annoyed but not surprised. He wanted her to believe him.

"Perhaps we can talk in my office. Away from Spoon City," Angelo stated. After hesitating, he turned his back on Norah to lead her to another part of the commercial kitchen. When she followed, he addressed the chef he'd splashed with soup.

"The bisque is exceptional, Chef."

The burst of pride that hit Norah in the back almost knocked her over. "Thank you, Chef!" the young woman cried.

Angelo's office was cramped and cool. The built-in bookshelves that lined two full walls were piled with jars, pots, terrariums, and fish tanks, making it look more like an apothecary shop than a chef's office. Something dark writhed in a jar in the far corner, and Norah grimaced.

Angelo noticed. "Kilomea eel pasta. It's going on the menu as soon as we get a ruling on whether it counts as vegetarian."

"Is the pasta animal?" Norah asked.

"That's the million-dollar question. It's taxonomically closer to a green bean, but it's more sentient than a goldfish."

"How does it rank against a television executive?" Norah muttered.

Angelo snorted, and Norah fixed him with a stern gaze. "Did you bake that cake that threatened my parents?"

Angelo shook his head.

Based on the emotions flowing from him, she was sure he was telling the truth. He wasn't telling her everything, but he bore her no ill will. "Do you know who did?"

"We had problems with the studio oven. That ridiculous, oversized custom thing. Big appliances, big problems. Buggy as a swamp. The set was crawling with electricians and builders. Any of them could have planted the cake."

"But you're the only person on Earth who uses impfruit."

Angelo cringed, and a current of embarrassment splashed out of him. "Is that what was in the cake?" He was lying.

"Oh, please. There's not a produce varietal on Earth or Oriceran you don't know about."

A short stab of pride hit Norah, which annoyed her. "I'm not flattering you. I'm accusing you."

"I may be the *best* magical-terrestrial chef on two worlds, but I'm not the *only* one."

Norah's eyes blazed. "You're the only one who was on the set when a layer cake threatened to murder my parents."

"Which makes me the perfect stooge." A current of shame and anger eddied around Angelo. Darkness pooled near his heart.

"What aren't you telling me?"

Angelo frowned. "That cake was a threat against me as much as you. My father is moving against me. Slowly, mind you. He's sous-viding me by inches, a contact here, a job there. He knows you're one of my greatest advocates. Or at least, you were."

Sorrow welled from Angelo's chest and washed over her. Norah clicked the radio magic off. She didn't need to feel worse.

"Who else could get impfruit?" she asked.

Angelo scratched his chin with an impeccably mani-cured hand.

"There's a stall at the Santa Monica farmers' market. Oriceran and Earth produce. Hybrids, too. I got an ostrich eggplant there a few weeks ago that made me believe in God again. If anyone had impfruit, they would."

The next market was two days from now. If Norah's trust was misplaced, she'd be in even hotter water.

"Norah," he began as she was about to leave. She turned.

"I catered a lunch for some executives the other day. And, uh, there's something you should know."

Norah raised an eyebrow. "Are you sure you're not breaking caterer-client confidentiality?"

Angelo seemed affronted but went on. "One of your

clients got cast on a show, right? A cheerful light elf. Ingénue type?"

"It's not to series yet, but yeah."

"And you two are romantically involved?"

Norah cringed. "Does everyone in Hollywood know about my love life?"

"Everyone who reads *US Weekly* does." He pulled an article up on his phone.

It was a photo of her and Frondle sun-beaming. Her legs were wrapped around him, and her face was stupid with admiration.

"Who took this? We were a thousand feet in the air!"

The drone. We almost crashed into that drone.

"Up-and-coming agent Norah Wintry and her light elf boy toy take their relationship to new heights."

The headline was *Magic in the Air.*

Norah gritted her teeth. "That's a great title."

"I know. The executives like the pilot, but they're not sure about Frondle. They think your feelings might have clouded your judgment."

"Shit. Part of why I like him is because he's talented. If I were a man dating an actor, no one would bat an eye."

"It's terrible to be judged for an accident of birth," Angelo stated pointedly. "I thought you should know."

Norah sighed. "Thanks. I'm not happy, but now I can do something about it."

They agreed to meet at the farmers' market on Wednesday, and Norah went to stew in her car.

When she returned to First Arret, she stopped downstairs at the pizza place. Ji-woo, who was working the counter, smiled brightly when he noticed her.

"I haven't seen you much. The kimchi ranch hasn't gone downhill, has it? Dad's been fiddling with the ferments. I found him singing to the jars." Ji-woo shook his head affectionately.

"No way. The kimchi's perfect. If you sold it in gallon jugs, I would bathe in it." She poked a small condiment jar that depicted a beaming Mr. Kim riding a red-and-white cow. "Add it to my order." She plunked it on the table." A few minutes later, she trudged upstairs with a large cheese pizza and a bag of garlic knots. Combined with the ranch, she hoped it would be a big enough bribe.

On the roof, a terrifying painting leaned against the stairwell egress. It was good to have a use for the magical Murphy bed, and she was glad to have it gone. Every time Norah saw the glittering grotesquerie, she found something new to be alarmed by. Today it was a small smiley face formed by the folds of the wrinkles on the screaming face.

Uriel, who had claimed the small pocket of space-time, sat cross-legged on a cushion in front of the painting, nose buried in his laptop. He had strung a clothesline between the painting and the side of the building, and his gray shirts were drying in the light breeze.

"You can move to my guest room if you want," Norah said.

Uriel shook his head without looking at her. "Conventional real estate is a tool of the oppressor."

"What *isn't* a tool of the oppressor?"

"Open-source code and jazz," Uriel replied, failing to pick up on her irony.

"You should talk to Nostril about that."

Uriel's fingers paused fractionally. "Nice kid." He kept typing.

"I need to ask you for a favor."

"If it's interesting, I'll consider it."

"I need to learn more about some television executives. Specifically, a guy named Bernard Montopolis. Can you hack into his calendar?"

"That's not interesting." Uriel had not stopped typing.

"Oh, come on. It's television. It's *sexy*!"

"Television is a tool of the oppressor. Toolier than most."

"'Toolier' isn't a word. It's a tiny job. Or can you not do it?" Norah fed faux skepticism into her voice.

Uriel didn't fall for it. "Mind games won't work on me. Psychology is another tool—"

"Of the oppressor," Norah finished. "Look, your code almost killed my parents. Get me the fucking schedule. Also, I brought pizza to bribe you." She waved the box.

He relented from guilt and hunger. As Norah gave him the executives' names and email addresses, he fiddled with an antenna near the edge of the roof, then ate two slices of pizza, then typed continuously for ten minutes. His fingers moved so fast that they occasionally disappeared.

"Those bougie idiots are as overscheduled as their eight-year-olds," he grumbled, turning his screen to face her. She scanned the schedule. There were a billion entries, but only a few that met her requirements. She scrolled until she landed on one of Bernard's lunch dates three days from now. It was at Musso and Frank. Go figure.

"Thanks," she said, but Uriel had already slid headphones over his ears and reattached his eyeballs to the bright rectangle of his screen. She stole a piece of the pizza she had bribed him with and doused it in ranch dressing as she dialed Frondle's number.

"I need to talk to you," she told him. "Will you meet me at Musso and Frank? Yeah, again."

CHAPTER TWELVE

On Wednesday, Norah met Angelo outside the Santa Monica farmers' market. The white peaks of the plastic tents looked like meringues under the blue sky, and the air smelled like flowers and tomatoes. Angelo was wearing a graphic comic book t-shirt, plaid leggings, Crocs, and a pink trucker hat that said TRUCKER.

"What are you wearing?" Norah asked, eyeballs assaulted by the clashing patterns.

"I'm undercover," Angelo informed her.

"As someone with no taste? The Crocs give you away as a chef."

"It was that or my alligator loafers, and I didn't want to bring the girls to the grubby Santa Monica streets."

"Ugh. If you're undercover as half a Buffalo Exchange, then I'm undercover as someone who wants to eat a lot of cheese samples." Norah plucked a camel's milk brie sample from a nearby table. Spreading it across a cracker, she chewed ostentatiously. "Oh, my God! Is this one hump or two?"

The cheesemonger, a small dark-haired woman perched on a wooden stool, sighed. "One. It's good, huh?"

"It's unbelievable. Where do you keep the camels?" Norah asked.

"We have a ranch in Calabasas. Take a card. Visit any time."

Angelo tugged her away, and Norah rolled her eyes. "I can't stop to eat *one* piece of cheese."

"That woman is a hack," Angelo informed her. "She feeds her camels grain! They should be grazers."

He glared over his shoulder. When the cheesemonger saw his face, her eyes narrowed.

"If you insist on insulting all your weird culinary rivals, you'll give us away," Norah grumbled.

"A man has his pride." Angelo huffed and crossed his arms.

Norah wandered over to a kiosk of jams, enjoying the revulsion on Angelo's face as she dipped pretzels in two or three and handed over a crisp twenty-dollar bill for a jar of apricot-lemon marmalade.

As she admired her purchase, Angelo began to hyper-ventilate. "They don't even make it themselves! They buy it from the supermarket, put it in second-hand mason jars, and quadruple the price."

"Good for them!" Norah stopped to smell a bouquet of flowers.

As she leaned in, a blossom swung out and hit her in the forehead. "Back off, lady. I don't go sticking my nose in your face."

Norah gazed at the empty space around her. The flower

seller was ten feet away, having a quiet conversation with a stylish young couple.

"You got a problem?" Norah finally identified the source. The flower was talking to her. Nestled in a colorful bouquet, the deep crimson rose's petals formed an irritated pout.

"It's a cantankerose, "Angelo whispered. The rose crossed two of its leaves over its stem and spat a drop of crystalline dew that splashed her shoe. "It's a flower for curmudgeons. And exes. Occasionally."

Norah liked it immensely, and when the flower seller was done with his quiet conversation, she approached him.

"I want to buy the cantankerose."

"Oh, great. You're not gonna put me in some frou-frou vase in a beautiful sunlit corner, are you?" the rose shouted from the table. "Disgusting."

"Be nice, or I'll feed you to my goat," Norah shot back.

"Nice try, lady, but I'd taste like bottled farts."

"I've seen him eat old gym shoes," Norah replied thoughtfully, to an uneasy silence.

"Are you sure?" the flower seller asked. "They can live for, like, three months. In my experience, most people get tired of the joke in, like, fifteen minutes."

"The joke's in your pants!" the rose shouted.

"I'm sure," Norah said. "Please?"

"It's your funeral," the flower seller replied. "You're not taking it to a funeral, are you?"

She shook her head and swiped her credit card while the cantankerose made fun of her outfit.

Angelo tugged on her arm. "There's the farm stand," he whispered. Norah turned.

The booth was enormous, and its white plastic awning had been replaced by light elf silk, its intricate woven amber-and-citrine whorls wafting on hand-carved poles. The tables beneath sagged with produce. Strange pale melons the size of basketballs hung from the awning, dripping with icicles. Woven baskets laden with cherries nestled against radioactively bright apples. A sunfruit tree planted in a wine barrel illuminated the back of the stall.

A dark-blue velvet cloth displayed root vegetables with silly half-human faces, bulbous noses and chubby cheeks. They were cute until one of them blinked.

"Where's the impfruit?" Norah whispered.

"I don't see it," Angelo said. "Let's get closer."

They moved slowly through the booth, stopping here and there to pretend to look at produce. Norah picked up a head of broccoli, and the flower under her arm shouted, "Broccoli? You're not gonna eat that. You're gonna buy it to feel better about yourself, then let it rot in the fridge."

Several other shoppers stared at her, smirking.

"I'm going to eat this broccoli to spite you." She tucked it under her arm with the flower. It would give her a good excuse to talk to the farm owner. "Now shut up, or I'm going to rip you to pieces and strew you across my bed in a romantic gesture," she whispered.

"I'd like to see you try," the rose snarled. She shushed it as they approached the center of the billowing silk tent.

Angelo made a show of prodding a nearby cucumber, which glittered with light like a jellyfish when his finger made contact. "That's Jed," he whispered, nodding the brim of his terrible hat toward the man running the kiosk. Jed sauntered over to them, his long, shaggy beard juxtaposed with an expensive outfit.

Jed wore farmer's clothes, or to be more accurate, he was dressed like someone attending a Met Gala with a farming theme. His leather overalls were beaded with colorful pop-art livestock, and he wore them over a shirt made from sheer light elf chiffon.

"What's it gonna take to get you into that cuke?" he asked cheerfully. Angelo kept his face down and muttered something unintelligible.

Jed's eyes grew sharp as his eyes darted from Angelo's chin to a small white scar that traced up the chef's index finger. He took a half-step back, and the temperature in the tent cooled by degrees. After a half-second's hesitation, he crooked a hand carefully toward the nearby potted sunfruit tree.

The root-packed soil ball that hurtled toward Norah's head at pro baseball speeds told her the man was an earth elemental. As she was about to raise a shield, Angelo pulled a thread of darkness out from under the nearest produce table and spun it into a broad net that guided the sunfruit tree to a gentle stop an inch from Norah's nose. Carefully grabbing the trunk, he set the tree back in its pot.

"What are you doing?" Norah asked.

"Those are ripe sunfruit!" Angelo cried, spinning in a broad circle as he searched for the farmer, who had used the distraction to run out.

"Ugh. A tree-hugger," an irate voice near Norah's armpit said. The cantankerose wiggled into the light and pointed a leaf. "Mr. Overalls went toward that keto bakery stand." Norah and Angelo sprinted to a small kiosk where attractive, muscular people picked at undersized and unappetizing bricks that vaguely resembled food.

There was a clatter of beads on the asphalt as their target exploded out from under the baker's stand and raced down the aisle. Angelo, sprinting behind him, crashed into the corner of the tent's display case. A basket of muffin-adjacent food balls exploded on the asphalt.

"You did that on purpose," Norah panted.

Angelo puffed up. "When a man sees an insult to his very way of life..." He was too out of breath to continue.

They pushed through throngs of shoppers, losing ground, and the smell of salt in the air grew stronger. That wasn't good.

"We have to stop him!" Norah shouted. Fighting an earth elemental on the beach would be like fighting a tiger in a pit full of additional tigers.

Two stunning spells missed their target by wide margins, and Jed leapt nimbly over the crackling blue magical trip line she extended at ankle level.

"It's too bright!" Angelo cried. Sunlight ricocheted off the road onto the shining stucco buildings, illuminating everything in sight. The meager squares of shade beneath the parked cars were the only sources of power he could access. He pulled one of these out, formed it into a rough ball, and lobbed it at the farmer, who was widening the gap. The ball burst at his feet, and he stumbled but caught the asphalt with a hand and scrambled to his feet.

A mannequin outside a cheesy gift shop in the distance gave Norah an idea. She shot a glamour out of sight along the asphalt. When the spell hit, the mannequin sprouted long brown hair, and its outfit transformed from a t-shirt that said MY OTHER CAR IS A BONG into practical navy blue yoga pants and a sports bra.

Not a perfect likeness, but good enough. *If Uriel can glamour dummies, so can I.*

When the earth elemental saw the Norah-mannequin raise its wand, he reeled in confusion. He stepped badly off the curb and sprawled flat on the road, then tendrils of darkness from under the nearest parked car wrapped around his wrists and ankles, keeping him down.

Jed shut his eyes, muscles stretching his skin tight. The asphalt he was bound to sprayed gravel as it broke free from the road in massive chunks. These lofted into the air like balloons as he sprinted, shedding dirt and tar. He raced between two buildings, and the asphalt chunk attached to his right leg swung wide into a dog walker. She screamed and tried to untangle her rainbow-dyed poodle as the asphalt skipped off a series of Teslas, denting their shining paint. He tried to make it around another corner, but the asphalt attached to his left hand hooked into a bike rack. As he untangled himself, Norah knocked him to the ground with an old-fashioned burst of raw magic. Angelo wasn't taking any chances this time, and strips of darkness laced across him until he looked like a film negative of a mummy.

"I'll get your dad his money, I swear." Jed's eyes widened as the chef laced a strip of darkness under his nose.

Angelo paused. "What money?"

Confusion mirrored confusion, and Norah flicked on her radio magic. Jed was terrified and ashamed. He wished he hadn't had to borrow so much money. He wished he could stop...something. Gambling? Drugs? Norah couldn't quite tell.

"He owes your dad money," she explained. "He thinks you're here to collect."

Angelo's emotions churned, and a burst of shame shot out from the crown of his head. Turning back to Jed, he removed a few of the more excessive straps of dark magic. Jed wiggled in his newfound millimeter of freedom.

"I don't work for my father anymore," Angelo told him.

"Yeah, right. You didn't chase me down to ask me about my blue filigree mushrooms."

"You have blue filigrees?" Menu ideas flickered in Angelo's eyes.

"He'd beat you up for mushrooms way before he'd beat you up for money." Norah poked Jed in a beaded chicken. The produce seller squirmed nervously.

Angelo grunted. "I don't want to beat you up. I do want to talk to you about those mushrooms…"

"Focus, Angelo!"

"Ahem. We're here to ask about recent impfruit sales."

"Impfruit? You don't want impfruit. That stuff tastes likes shit. It's worse than durian," Jed snapped.

"I like durian."

"No one likes durian. People say they do because Bourdain liked it. I think Bourdain was punking us."

"You can debate the merits of stinky-foot melon later," Norah told them. "Tell us about the impfruit."

"We don't have any."

"Who does?" Norah asked. Two people had stopped to gawk near the mouth of the alley, and she wanted to hurry things up.

"The customer we sold our last stock to might be reselling it," Jed told them. "You could ask them."

"You sold some?" Norah asked.

"Yeah."

"To whom?"

"I don't know. Morin was working the booth that day. She'd know more than me. We switch market days."

Norah crouched near Jed's face. "That's great. So, where's Morin?"

Jed shivered. "She's at the farm. Unless she's making a supply run, she's always at the farm."

The shiny corner of a business card stuck out of Jed's front pocket. As Norah snagged it, a beaded sheep on Jed's bib shed its embellished wool onto the pavement. Jed groaned.

"That was couture. Someone did the beadwork by hand."

That's what you get for wearing couture to a farmers' market.

"Sorry," Norah said cheerfully, reading the address on the card. "Ooh! Ojai. I love their energy vortex."

"So do the jelly cukes." Jed slumped. Angelo set Jed's bonds to dissolve in two minutes, and they put their heads together as they high-tailed it out of Santa Monica.

"Do you want to go now?"

Norah shook her head. "No. I know the perfect people to help me investigate a farm, but I'll have to ask them to drive from the Bay. I have some business with Frondle to take care of first."

CHAPTER THIRTEEN

Norah picked the fight halfway through her chicken parmesan.

"You care more about your stupid light elf honor than you do about me!"

Frondle downed the rest of his martini and slammed it on the table in disgruntlement. Then he broke out in a hacking cough while he fished the toothpick from his olive out of the back of his throat. Norah would have laughed, but now was not the time.

"That toothpick has touched you more than I have over the past month." A man and a woman at a nearby table who were about to start a fight of their own checked her out with interest.

"I have to focus on my career right now. I'm too tall to play humans, and there aren't that many roles for elves."

"Career, career, career. Is that all I am to you? A rung on the ladder? Step on me until you reach the next rung?"

"Step on you and reach what? Another audition for a

community theater production of *A Midsummer Night's Dream?*" Frondle shouted.

He hesitated, and Norah gave him a microscopic smile of encouragement.

They'd been seated on the opposite side of the restaurant from Bernard and his executive posse. Norah had attempted to bribe the maître d' for a closer table with a twenty-dollar bill, and he'd given it a death glare that had withered every plant in a two-mile radius. Even the succulents. She didn't have more cash, and he didn't know what Venmo was, so she'd decided they would have to deal. Bribes had gotten expensive.

The farther you are from your audience, the bigger you have to play. Norah sprang to her feet and pulled her coat off its hook with such force that it swung across a nearby table, splitting a puddle of bearnaise down the middle and knocking a highball into an elegantly-dressed dark elf's lap.

"I am *so* sorry," she cried. Frondle made a hand gesture indicating that she was speaking too quietly. *"I AM SO SORRY,"* she repeated, and the dark elf edged away from her. Satisfied, she turned back to Frondle. "This is all your fault. Look at this!" She held the bearnaise-drenched corner of the coat up for him to inspect. Confused, he leaned in to lick the sauce off. Feeling this was a bridge too far, she yanked the coat away and sharply shook her head.

Norah strode in the direction of Bernard's table and grabbed a server by the red-coated arm.

"Excuse me. I need your help!"

If this doesn't work, we're doomed.

Bernard's head turned in her direction. *Finally.* Norah fixed her eyes on the elderly white-gloved server whose arm she still held. "I need your help. My stupid date spilled our drinks."

All eyes in the room drilled into her, and Norah forced herself to breathe. There was a reason she hadn't gone into performance. Bernard's eyes tracked her as she stomped back to her table.

"Put everything on my tab. That table's lunch, too. It's *his* fault," she cried, pointing at Frondle. "He should be the one paying, but *he* doesn't have any money." She made a show of forcing a credit card on the server as Frondle sprang out from behind the table. Holding the room's attention made him more confident, and his eyes sparkled with enjoyment.

"I would have money if you were a better agent."

Norah tried to gasp dramatically, but a droplet of spittle went down her windpipe, and she ended up coughing for several seconds instead. Swiping a water from a shocked couple's table, she downed it in a gulp and flung the glass aside.

"I got you that gig as Prince Charming, and you quit!"

"Playing make-believe at children's birthdays was beneath me as an actor!" Frondle cried, managing to be both dignified and ear-shatteringly loud. He was good at this.

When Frondle had first moved to Los Angeles, he *had* worked a few parties as Prince Charming and had rather enjoyed it. Children loved his wide-eyed enthusiasm. *I wonder if he's as good with sentient signage as he is with kids?*

It was time to go in for the kill. "Beneath you as an actor? You're not an actor! You're an unemployed barista!" Red and screaming, she stormed out of the restaurant, jostling as many tables as she could on the way out.

When she'd put a full three blocks between her and the scene she'd caused, the scowl on her face disappeared, though her adrenaline stayed high. That had gone well. If it helped Frondle, humiliating herself for the Hollywood glitterati would be worth it.

She hopped into her Prius to wait. Fifteen minutes later, Frondle slipped in beside her.

"I picked at my linguini like you said. Very morosely."

He showed her his puppy-dog expression, and she laughed. "Did Bernard say anything to you?" Norah asked.

"No, but he was watching me."

"Good." She put the car in gear and pointed it toward Los Feliz. When she parked at her apartment, Frondle loitered in the car, face uncertain.

"What is it?" Norah asked.

"Do you really think I'm not an actor? That I'm a failed barista?"

"What? No! That was for show," Norah told him. His blue eyes sparkled in the hazy light, and her heart went into overdrive.

"I think you're good, and you're getting even better." She kissed him. She couldn't help herself. Frondle's tense face softened, and Norah pulled away before he could say anything about his honor.

"What do you think? Do I have a career in the theater?" she asked.

"When you try, you're very loud," Frondle told her enthusiastically. "Does that count?" His hand slid across her back and under her shirt. His skin burned, and she was still amped on adrenaline. She thought she would burst. She attempted to crawl into his lap, but he was so tall that he was practically folded in half in the Prius's small passenger seat. They twisted themselves into pretzels trying to get their hands on each other.

A loud knock on the window sent them springing away from one another as if a magnetic force inside the car had been reversed. It was Billy.

Frondle, clearly embarrassed, made a show of searching the glove compartment.

I forgot to stock up on plausible excuses.

Norah cracked her door, ignoring Frondle's agitation.

"Hey." Billy's tone suggested that he regretted knocking.

"What's up?" Norah asked. She attempted to fasten a loose button before realizing it had popped off the shirt.

"If you two aren't busy…well, it looks like you are. Uh..."

"We're not busy." Frondle selected a random item from the glove compartment and waved it in the air with a triumphant "Aha!"

It was a receipt for medicated dandruff shampoo. Frondle read it and frowned.

"I bought that for Pepe." She snatched it, a blush creeping up her cheeks.

Billy diligently studied an empty spot near the horizon. "Um. The thing is, Stan's gone, and he asked me to take care of the draconewts in the pool. They're out of control."

"What are you talking about?" Norah asked.

Billy scratched under the collar of his t-shirt. "The draconewts? Little red amphibians? It's important to remember that they eat a *lot* of mosquitos. No one in this complex will be getting malaria. Or dengue fever. That's for sure."

As Billy sang the draconewts' praises, a tendril of smoke rose over the pool area.

"Oh, shit." Billy sprinted toward the complex.

"Snuffing out smoldering fires. How appropriate," Norah muttered, casting a glance at Frondle as she trailed after Billy. *We can stand under the sprinklers when we're done.*

Norah assumed it would be difficult to set an aloe plant on fire, but as the smoking borders of the turquoise blue pool unfurled before her, she decided she'd underestimated the enemy.

Water splashed on the indigo deck tiles as Billy upended a bucket on a smoking terracotta pot. There was a flash of red, and a bulbous head peeked out from behind a coiled green hose. From nose to tail, the creature was almost a foot long. Its skin was a porous matte black underscored by glowing orange, and its eyes were covered by smoky-quartz lids.

"For a newt, it doesn't look very slimy." Norah unspooled the hose and turned on the water. She gripped it like a gunfighter and checked the surroundings. There was a yelp behind her. Frondle had caught one of the draconewts under a bowl-sized hemisphere of woven sunlight.

Billy coughed. "They're not slimy because they're not amphibious in air and water."

"Then where do they live?" Norah asked, aiming the nozzle at a pair of glowing eyes under a glossy green-leafed tree. The newt raised its head and pulled a fat fly into its gullet with a thin tongue. When it swallowed, a faint rumble rose from its body. Norah leaned to identify the source of the noise. Up close, its skin resembled solidified lava.

The draconewt belched, and a fiery strip of pain shot across Norah's face. She smelled burning hair a moment before she identified the source as her eyebrow and shrieked as she blasted her face with the hose nozzle. The spray shot into her sinuses and she quickly diverted it, dripping long trails of water and snot.

Frondle appeared to be having an aneurysm. He shook and brought his hand to his mouth. She was about to work a diagnostic spell when he threw his head back and burst out laughing. Several nearby newts croaked in unison. Billy took the opportunity to stun them, then stuffed their bodies into a large fireproof sack.

"The draconewts don't live in air and water. They live in air and lava," he explained apologetically.

Norah, touching smooth red skin where her eyebrow had been, spun to the garden, hose in hand. The draconewts would pay. Frondle pulled himself together and moved into formation behind her as she moved through the garden like an assassin, casting rapid-fire stunning spells at anything that moved. When a particularly fast or bold newt escaped the flash of her wand, Frondle caught it in a net of golden light.

"How come I've never noticed fire-breathing newts in the pool?" she asked Billy, touching her eyebrow again.

"They don't start breathing fire until they're two months old. Stan took care of them before then."

"Then he decided to flee to Antarctica and let the place burn?" Norah banked a stun spell off a small reflector disk into the depths of a drainage pipe. It hit with a satisfying hiss, and she yanked the retreating draconewt out by an ankle.

"I was supposed to round them up and take them to Stan's unicorn-feed guy last week."

The newt in Norah's hand gazed at her with sorrowful lambent eyes.

"They feed these things to unicorns?" she asked.

"Don't be ridiculous. I'm sure they grind them up first."

The draconewt emitted a soft *meep*, and smoke curled adorably over its face.

"Sorry, buddy." Norah guiltily threw it into Billy's sack.

"That's why I kept putting it off. Have you met a unicorn? They're assholes, and they smell like roadkill." They weren't Norah's favorites either. "And these little dudes have done a war-crimes-level massacre on the local mosquito population." Billy plucked a stunned draconewt out of a smoking aloe bush. Norah spritzed the vegetation as he contemplated the newt.

"You're a good little dragon, aren't you?"

The stunned newt's eyes narrowed, and Billy dropped him into the sack.

Something bleated near ground level, and Pepe trotted around the corner. Red flashed on his black fur, and Norah jumped when she realized a small draconewt was riding on Pepe's back with a Napoleonic expression on its face.

"Don't. Move," Norah said, aiming her wand.

Pepe bleated an objection and sidestepped the spell as it left her wand. The newt on his back bellowed and spat a marble-sized fireball into a nearby daffodil planter. Pepe trotted over, stamped out the smoking daffodil, ate the charred remains, and bleated again.

Blond hair rustled against the vegetation as Frondle, crouched, crept up on the pair with a net of light between his hands. He raised an eyebrow at Norah. When she nodded, he dropped the net on the animals. Pepe bleated, and Norah swore that for one second, his eyes flashed white. The net of light exploded into a flock of butterflies that fluttered away in all directions. Norah coughed and plucked one of the butterflies from the air. It appeared to be a normal insect.

"What the hell was that?" Norah asked, frightened.

Frondle, looking serious, rolled a ball of explosive light between his palms, eyeing the goat. That failed to impress Pepe, who bleated in annoyance and curled up in his favorite spot in the hydrangeas. His draconewt rider lazily scanned its opponents, made three small circles on Pepe's wiry hair, and fell asleep.

"What is the deal with that goat?" Billy asked.

Pepe's soft snore was echoed by the draconewt, who emitted a single flame like a candle as he or she slept.

"I don't know," Norah said. "But one, I don't think he's a goat, and two, he adopted a runty fire hazard as his familiar."

CHAPTER FOURTEEN

An investigation into Pepe's true nature was on Norah's to-do list, but it was at the bottom, next to non-essentials like washing her shower curtain and flossing. She threw herself into work again, pleased that at least Duncan was making a steady income.

When Sid and Castor dropped by that afternoon, they found her refilling Floe bottles from the bathroom tap. *Stupid Norah. Always lock the door before you commit petty fraud.*

"Uh..."

Sid's eyebrows twisted together as he stared at the half-full bottle in her hand. Given the expression on his face, he probably saw it as half-empty. "I've told many people that Floe tastes identical to regular LA tap water. Do they think I'm a fraud? Do they talk about how I've lied about drinking real Floe? Maybe I *should* buy a real bottle to check."

Castor rolled his eyes and plucked the bottle from her

hand. "Smart and eco-friendly! Floe is notorious for depleting critical community aquifers."

"Thank you, Castor," Norah said pointedly. Sid was staring at a droplet sliding down the side of the bottle.

"Sid, relax. First, when people talk about you, which isn't often, they talk about your emails. Second, Floe *does* taste like regular tap water. That's how I get away with it. I think I have a real bottle somewhere in the office if you're that upset about it."

She waved away his protests about any taste test having to be double-blind and loaded them up with full bottles for the walk back down the hall.

She didn't see Stellan in the corner chair of the lobby until it was too late.

"You!" The dwarf jabbed a stubby finger at Castor as he leapt to his feet. The wizard stumbled back against the doorframe.

Stellan, whose beard was a sleek red waterfall, grabbed the room's floor lamp and homed in on the cowering wizard. The cord crackled with electricity near Stellan's thick boots. There was a tremendous crash and splash as half the bottles in Castor's arms broke, raining Floe on the carpet.

Shoddy overpriced elitist manufacturing.

Stellan crunched through the bottle shards as if they were leaves, swinging the lamp in a lazy circle.

"You fucked with my props. That monster was my baby." His voice grew softer and angrier. He raised the lamp, and Castor threw an unbroken bottle of Floe at him. Stellan connected with it like a baseball, and a slurry of water and glass hit Norah's ankles.

"If you're going to fight, can you do it with something cheaper than Floe? I could go to Ralph's and get some store-brand seltzer." Norah dashed over to unplug the cord from the wall before the pooling water reached it.

Stellan turned, and his sleek, shiny beard reflected a rough outline of her face. Glass crunched as he took two swift, menacing steps toward her. "Why is that little shitbag here? And his prevaricating friend? The answer had better be because you've set a devious trap and have a gruesome magical punishment in store for them."

"I'm sure that forcing them to write screenplays with each other counts as a devious magical punishment." She said it lightly, but the last flicker of good humor disappeared from Stellan's face. His next half-hearted swing was easily dodged as he spun on Castor. "I should stuff cursed marionette eyes into *your* face. See how *you* like it!" Fury blazed in his eyes as he tracked Castor's retreat. "Hey, Norah, do you have a melonballer?"

"In my office?" Norah threw a magical shield in front of the young wizard before the lamp made contact. The shade flew off, and the bulb underneath smashed against the crackling blue magic, raining yet more glass on her waiting room's carpet. She had picked the wrong day to wear open-toed mules.

Castor shrank, disentangled his wand from his pocket, and cast a shaky stunning spell. The line of rust-red magic zoomed toward Stellan, and Norah was about to relax when the magic bounced off the dwarf's shining beard and shot back into Castor's face. Stiffening, the wizard wobbled on his feet until Stellan stalked up and poked his chest with a single fat finger. Castor toppled onto the wet glass-covered floor.

"How did you do that?" Norah asked, mesmerized by the length of silky beard.

"The witch who does my Brazilian blowouts added anti-stunning serum."

A red trickle of blood threaded across the floor from under Castor, and Norah raised her wand for real. "If you came here to threaten my clients, you've succeeded."

"With clients like these, you don't need enemies," Stellan replied. "I came here to invite you to a welcome home party for Stan, but consider that invitation rescinded."

He tossed the lamp on the floor, spat at Castor, and strode out, grinding glass into the carpet as he went. When he was gone, Norah warded the door with her beefiest padlock rune. She didn't need drop-ins seeing First Arret clients bleeding out on the carpet.

Castor groaned when she un-stunned his face and crouched beside him. "I'm going to leave you frozen while I find out where this blood is coming from." After summoning the broken glass off the floor and dumping it in a pile to deal with later, she rolled Castor onto his side. A large shard of glass stuck out of his lower back below his kidney.

Norah traced a painkilling rune on Castor's skin, then carefully slid the shard out as she hit the area with a healing spell. Castor gasped as his skin knitted together in a shiny pink scar.

"What the fuck is going on in here?" A gravelly voice, weirdly metallic, echoed from a grate in the ceiling. A thin line of magic cut a hole in the grate, and Madge popped into the room, breathing hard.

"Why is the door warded?" She noticed Castor on the floor. "Oh, shit."

"Yeah. We're going to have to buy lots of new bottles of Floe." Norah almost cried when she thought about the size of the Erewhon bill.

Madge glanced at Sid, then flew down and helped Norah pull shards out of Castor. She was especially useful on the smaller chunks. Castor's continuous whimper during this process was so high-pitched that Norah wished she had left him stunned.

"You know, the business is doing well enough that we could buy real Floe." Madge gritted her teeth and braced her feet against Castor's face as she pulled a truculent sliver out of his shoulder.

Norah hit the bleeding puncture with a coagulation spell.

When she reversed the remaining stunning spell, Castor curled into a ball against the wall, his face a few shades paler than untrammeled snow. Norah retrieved her blue leather jacket from a peg on the wall and dropped it over his shoulders after checking to make sure he wasn't bleeding egregiously.

Her phone rang insistently, and she would have ignored it if she hadn't seen the number. It was Dakota, the *Green & Pointy* casting assistant.

"Shit. Can you make sure he doesn't keel over, Madge? I have to take this."

Shutting her office door, she took a deep breath. "Dakota! How's it going?"

"Norah, hey." The subsequent pause was so long that Norah thought the call had dropped. Finally, however, there was a cough. "I... This is awkward, but I heard about Musso and Frank."

"Oh, no. I didn't mean for anyone else to hear us," she lied, pumping her fist in secret triumph.

"Eh. I'd bet money that place sees two breakups a day. Apparently, Bernard found it very entertaining. Anyway, that's what I called to talk about. Sort of."

"Okay." Norah leaned toward the earpiece.

"Now that you two have broken up, what's the real skinny on Frondle? Are you going to keep repping him?

The plan had worked. This was her big moment. "I hate Frondle." Norah sighed dramatically. She let the pause hang for a count of three, fidgeting with an earring. *I am not cut out for this.* "I hate Frondle because he broke my heart, but he's too talented to drop."

"Really? He's not, you know, only a face?"

"Sadly, he's much more. I'd love to send him packing back to whatever the Oriceran equivalent of Kansas is, but I'd be shooting myself in the foot." She managed to sound sincere.

Dakota was almost, but not quite, convinced. "You're sure?"

"I'm sure."

"A hundred percent?"

Norah grinned. "A hundred and ten."

"Okay. That's good since the network bought twelve episodes. Mal's onboard, and if you're *really* sure, we're going to keep Frondle."

"I'm sure. The surest. He'll be great." Her heart soared. Twelve wasn't twenty-two, but it was good.

"If I can offer you some advice," Dakota said, "don't ride them too hard during negotiations. Bernard's still on the fence about Frondle, and you might scare him off."

With that, she hung up.

Norah burst back into the waiting room, spirits only slightly dampened by the bloody paper towel Madge was using to clean the blood off Castor's face.

"We've got a show!" she cried.

Madge whooped and accidentally punched Castor in the face. He rubbed his cheek, looking jealous.

"Frondle is going to be very happy."

"Happy enough to break an elven oath?" Madge asked, flying up to elbow Norah in the side.

It was possible. "I'm going to go tell him in person," Norah announced breathlessly.

"We haven't told you about our screenplay," Sid whined.

"Of all people, Sid, you should know about a little thing called email." She swanned out the door.

CHAPTER FIFTEEN

Norah nervously adjusted the straps of the overalls she'd purchased at her favorite thrift store. "How do I look? Do I look like a farmer? I modeled this outfit on the cover of *The Grapes of Wrath*."

Norah's father eyed the cluster of grapes in her hand. "Little on the nose?"

Norah chewed and groaned. "This isn't a prop. It's a snack for the car. The book made me hungry for grapes."

"Have you *read The Grapes of Wrath?*" Petra asked good-humoredly.

I've read Steinbeck's Wikipedia page. "Of course," Norah said primly.

"It's not about grapes," Lincoln added.

"Ugh. You're farmers. Sort of. What do farmers look like?"

Petra and Lincoln assessed one another. They both wore sturdy jeans and stained t-shirts.

"Like this, but with more goat poop." Petra touched the edge of her pristine shirt. Lincoln nodded enthusiastically.

"I can rub some dirt on you if you want." Norah reached toward the nearest potted plant.

"Farmers can do laundry like everyone else," Lincoln said. "What do you want your cover name to be? I wanted to be Maximillian, but your mother recommended something less ostentatious."

"I'm not going to need a cover." Norah rolled her eyes.

Norah's parents had contacted Morin under the guise of promoting a small farms collective. That was a real thing. Her parents ran it for a collection of small farmers throughout California.

"Does using the collective as a cover for an investigation cheapen it?" Lincoln asked.

Petra scoffed. "Well, we're the co-presidents of the collective. Keeping us alive is critical collective business."

"Hmmm. I suppose you're right. As usual." Lincoln smiled indulgently. Petra rolled her eyes.

"I still think we should have brought Pepe," Norah said. "To keep an eye on him, if nothing else."

"That creature is uncanny," Lincoln grumbled.

They bundled into the car for the drive up to Ojai. Sitting in the back was like being twelve again. Norah's parents asked her increasingly detailed questions about First Arret until she suggested they listen to an album by a client she was considering. That bought her an hour free from grilling.

"How *is* the goat farm holding up?" she finally asked. "You've both been here so much."

"We hired an extremely competent young woman from UC Davis with dual degrees in agricultural engineering and business," Petra said.

"I told your mother she was overqualified. She'd probably leave us immediately to be the CEO of Monsanto or something," Lincoln replied gruffly.

"She likes the goats. Monsanto can't compete with adorable goats."

"Hm. That's true. Anyway, the cheese sells for more than its weight in gold at fancy San Francisco grocery stores, so we must be doing something right."

When they got near Ojai, citrus groves dotted the horizon. They turned down a small gravel road under a sign that said Elemento Farm & Fishery. The road cut through a patchwork of fields blooming in bright colors. The jelly cukes were more spectacular on the vine than they were at the farm stand, and Norah resisted an urge to ask her dad to stop so she could watch the pretty colors. There were conventional vegetables here and there, too. At least, they seemed conventional from the road.

They pulled up at a collection of quaint farm buildings, including a big red barn out of a children's picture book. Lincoln crunched across the dirt toward the side of a farmhouse, where metal equipment rusted in the shade. With a few assessing tut-tuts, he poked at a spot of rust on the furrow below the handles. Similar farm equipment appeared in fifteenth-century woodcuts.

Petra, alert to movement, peered past the farmhouse into the barn's dark interior.

"Do they have livestock?" Norah asked.

"They farm tilapia," Petra said. "Which are basically swimming trashcans."

A small figure emerged from behind a shed, waving as she approached. The woman, who was in her mid-forties, had stringy brown hair tied up in a yellow bandana that made her skin look sallow. Her smile was perfunctory, and her deep blue eyes were cold. In contrast to Jed's couture, she wore ordinary overalls under muddy rubber boots.

"Hey! You folks are from the Caprini collective?"

"That's us." Petra nodded. "Pleasure to meet you. I'm Berenice. This is my husband Ron and our daughter...Glorah."

Norah glared at her mother. "That's me. Glorah."

"Interesting name," the woman said.

"It's German," Norah lied.

"Hm. I'm Morin." There was a round of handshakes and some commentary about the weather, which for farmers counted as shop talk. Morin's gaze lingered on Petra, and a faint line appeared between her eyebrows, but she shook her head.

"Why don't I start you off in the hothouse? That'll give you a sense of how I run things here." She motioned at a large, plastic-covered structure in the distance.

"Sounds great!" Petra ran a hand through her hair.

As they walked, the frown on Morin's face disappeared. She turned toward Lincoln, eyes searching his face above a plastered smile. "You do goats, right?"

"Yes. We have about a hundred, but we've got all kinds of agriculture in the collective. Ducks. We have a llama guy. One woman only grows Oriceran basil."

Morin glanced over her shoulder with a glint in her eyes. Norah's wand hand itched. *Is this a trap?*

The field to the right of the road to the hothouse was overgrown with moss. It was out of place in the California sun, not least because of its color. The carpet of vegetation was an eyewatering bright fuchsia, dotted with clusters of ivory pods that hung from underneath the leaves like grasping hands. A cotton candy smell wafted up the ground.

"Is that Pink Fairy?" Norah asked.

Petra winced, and Morin glanced at her.

Nice going, Glorah. Way to blow your cover.

"We're in here," Morin said, ignoring Norah's question and pointing at a vestibule covered in semi-transparent plastic. When they pushed through, the air inside the hothouse was so dense with vapor that Norah couldn't see the far side of the structure. The greenery was chaos, and much of it wasn't even green. She kept an eye out for impfruit, which Angelo said resembled a cross between a banana and a ram's horn.

A plastic shed sat to the left of the entrance, and past it was a crabapple tree, or part of one. Dark vines wrapped around the trunk. While the lower branches were heavy with familiar knobs of fruit, the upper half of the tree was choked by black vines. These, shiny and shot through with streaks of white, twisted into a nest where a cluster of seed pods pulsed darkly. It was unsettling.

"The chokepods are eye-catching, huh?" Morin asked. Norah nodded. She was about to ask what chokepods did when Morin added, "Let me show you something better." The farmer stepped to the shed. As the door cracked open, a cold weight settled in Norah's stomach. Metal inside flashed and her hand went to her wand, then relaxed when the image resolved.

It was a collection of well-organized gardening tools,

lifeless and polished. Lincoln perked up, nodding approvingly at a well-cared-for trowel.

Morin glanced at Norah's hand, which covered the end of the blue gum eucalyptus wand poking out of her pocket. Morin turned from Petra to Lincoln.

"What did you want to show us?" Norah asked.

Morin smiled brightly. "This." She raised her right hand, mouth distorted into a sickening smile. Three fingers twitched, and a trowel, rake, and pair of shears leapt off their hooks and hurtled toward them at lightning speed.

Shit. Morin was a metal elemental. It was unexpected from a farmer, but that was what you got for making assumptions.

Norah closed her fingers around her wand quickly enough to raise a wobbly blue shield. The trowel hit the magic surface and sparked, then spun in a tight arc as it slipped behind her back. Petra dropped, rolled, and snatched the wooden rake handle from the air. Lincoln, who had dropped his guard upon seeing the shed's impeccable organization, screamed. As Norah tracked the trowel, her father dropped to his knees, blood draining into the soil. The garden shears stuck out of his forearm, piercing the gap between the radius and the ulna.

"Dad!" Norah whirled aside an instant before the sharp end of the attacking trowel became intimately acquainted with her spinal cord.

A dive behind an upturned wheelbarrow brought her no closer to safety since the convex metal conveyance rose and slammed her into the damp soil. The edge of the basket pressed against her forearm, and she almost lost her grip on her wand.

Petra, still standing, struggled with the rake, pushing away the encroaching metal as the points inched toward her wide eyes.

The wheelbarrow pressed down and Norah screamed, then kicked the metal away with one foot as she shot three successive stunning spells at Morin. The farmer dodged and the spells missed, but it was enough of a distraction that the wheelbarrow tumbled off as Norah kicked it aside and dove for the gardening trowel. She ran to her father, yanked the shears from his arm, and traced a quick and dirty healing rune on his skin. The four puncture wounds didn't close, but they stopped bleeding. Lincoln, pale, gripped his wand in his off-hand.

"She recognized our faces," he whispered as Petra joined them and threw up a wide dome of protective green magical netting around all three of them. "Maybe she knows more about goats than we realized?"

"I don't think so," Petra said as Morin stalked toward a row of tomato plants along the far wall. She raised both hands and the metal stakes flew up, shedding moist soil as they rocketed toward Petra's protective net. Norah blocked the first handful and the dome blocked the stragglers. Lincoln finally went on the offense, raising to his knees and summoning a sparking ball of energy in his fist.

"So, what? Someone tipped her off that we were looking for impfruit?" Norah asked, picking off a stake headed for a gap in the net.

Lincoln, who was colorless, panted. "No. I think she recognized us from our profiles."

"Your profiles where?" Norah asked as the pace of the incoming projectiles exceeded her capacity to block them.

Lincoln breathed hard. "Our profiles on Dark Hound," He heaved the energy ball. Morin was focused on summoning stakes from the ground, and the magic grenade caught her off-guard and blasted her through the plastic hothouse wall. The tomato-stake barrage ceased.

Morin's small figure failed to reappear in the flapping hole. The suffocating vapor diffused into the morning sunlight, and Norah thought they were in the clear until the metal hoops holding the hothouse aloft rose in unison and slammed flat against the ground. Muggy plastic enveloped Petra's protective dome, and they were blind in a sea of semi-opaque tarp.

Norah drew a wide circle with her wand and filled it with the rune for fire. The plastic above them melted and curled back in a haze of acrid smoke. The sunlight beat down now, and Petra dropped the protective dome. All around them, loose plastic was settling down, blocking their view.

Mania glinted in Norah's eyes as she turned to her mother. "Fly me, Mom?"

"My pleasure, dear." Petra pushed up her sleeves and shot a dose of antigrav magic at the ground. As it filled Norah's tennis shoes, she shot into the air, finally able to search her surroundings for the fleeing metal elemental.

At the top of a lazy aerial arc, the farm came into focus. Idyllic in the sunlight, there only one tiny ball of movement—Morin, racing toward a series of large metal vats to the west of the buildings. Norah landed hard, rolled twice, and lost sight of her target in the scramble to regain her footing. It was time for the emotional radar. Sprinting toward the vats, she flicked on the knot of radio magic to its highest setting.

There! A flicker of desperation reached her. Morin wanted to *run run run*. Norah could feel her as she closed the distance between them, but when she reached the first of the metal vats, she couldn't see her target.

The vats must be for the fish. Clusters of shallow emotion pulsed inside them, rippling with faint excitement as her shadow fell over the water. The young tilapia thought it was lunchtime. *Sorry, buds.* A cold, killing desire drifted to Norah from the flat rectangle of a pond in the distance, and Norah homed in. *Morin.*

She strode toward the water, where agitated ripples lapped the damp grass along the shore.

The tilapia pond was a long rectangle, with ugly muddy water under plastic hoops that reined in bright green water lettuce. The grass was trampled near the edge, and a clump of torn vegetation lay limply on the bank. Norah recognized the Oriceran bubblegrass from photographs. If you ate it, you submerge for thirty minutes at a stretch without needing to breathe.

A fish splashed out in the lake, and a ball of cold killing instinct swam lazily toward her, pinging her radio. It was Morin, abandoning flight for fight.

Norah waded knee-deep into the water, pretending to look around in confusion as her internal radar tracked Morin's stalking approach. The pond was shallow. At any minute, dark, stringy hair would rise from the water.

Water rippled against her ankles, and a pair of eyes surfaced, pale green with slitted pupils.

When did Morin get slitted pupils? A caveman instinct lodged in her brainstem screamed in alarm.

Norah stumbled as the alligator opened its mouth, its sharp white teeth glinting with streaming water. As she fell backward, she sent a half-formed stunning spell in front of her by instinct. The blue magic barely penetrated the gator's skin, but the crush of the jaws slowed fractionally as the paleolithic impulse to kill overpowered Norah's emotions.

There was a burst of joy from the vats, but Norah only had an instant to recognize it as Morin since the gator was still coming. The first stunning spell had slowed it, and Norah shot a second into the deathly promise of its gullet. Its needle-sharp teeth broke her skin as the second spell took hold, leaving Norah rigid with fear on the bank. The gator sank lifelessly into the water as Norah yanked its jaws open and retrieved her bleeding leg. A loud splash behind her was followed by a scream of "Lovey!"

"Who the fuck is Lovey?" Norah asked between gritted teeth as Morin clambered over the edge of a nearby vat. Green water lettuce nestled in her stringy hair, and she raised her hands above her head.

"Please! You can kill me if you want, but let me pull Lovey from the water before she drowns."

"The alligator's name is *Lovey*?" Norah asked as Morin edged toward the shore.

"It's short for Gator Lovelace."

"What?"

"You know, like Ada Lovelace?" Morin whispered, eyeing Norah's blank expression. "The computing pioneer?"

"Stop!" The business end of Norah's wand twitched. "As much as I appreciate the history lesson, your alligator tried to murder me."

"She's an alligator! It's not her fault!" Morin splashed into the water. Exerting herself, she dragged the first four feet of the massive reptile onto the shore. Norah, who had experienced the gator's cold hunger for death first-hand, was unconvinced that this display of affection was warranted.

"You can do whatever you want with me now," Morin said.

"Okay." Norah fired her sturdiest stunning spell into the farmer's guts.

Breaking into the farmhouse turned out to be a challenge since it was locked with bolts that could only be manipulated from the inside. This was a popular security technique among metal elementals. When a range of spells failed to spring open the heavy wood, Norah emitted a soft string of curses and blasted a large hole in the nearest wall.

"Don't waste *all* your energy, dear," Petra pleaded.

"We're in Ojai. I'll sip a little vortex before we leave."

When they carried Morin's board of a body through the hole, she pulsed with an anger that rivaled Lovey's killing rage. They deposited her on the black-and-white tile floor of the dusty kitchen, and Petra, who had finally surfaced from the sea of plastic tenting, set to making tea. After a few seconds of rifling through the cupboards, she groaned.

"A farm full of rare Oriceran herbs, and they're drinking Lipton," she muttered, tossing tea bags into mugs. The legs of a metal chair scraped across the tile as Lincoln pulled up next to Morin, sat, and tapped her lips with his wand.

"I knew you weren't farmers," she sputtered. "Your shirts are way too clean."

Petra filled the kettle and placed it on the range. "It's called bleach, dear. You can work in a barn without acting like you were raised in one."

"See!" Norah said. "I wanted to rub dirt into their shirts," she whispered to Morin, claiming the good cop role.

"I take it you recognized us," Lincoln said.

Petra emitted a small, affronted noise. "We're less transparent in person than on your little antisocial media page."

Morin pressed her lips together.

"I understand how an earth elemental would wind up farming, but a metal elemental? I don't get it," Norah said.

"A plow is made of metal. A tractor is made of metal. A sprinkler is made of metal." Morin sounded bored.

"The dwarves have those weird copper trees they make novelty leaf armor out of," Lincoln mused.

The kettle whistled, and Petra pulled it off the stove. Bypassing the mugs, she let the spout dangle over the thin strip of ankle between Morin's tennis shoes and jeans.

"Dear, would you pull up Dark Hound?" Petra asked, touching Lincoln's upper arm. He put his reading glasses over his eyes and read his phone. A single drop of steaming water sloshed onto Morin's ankle, and her dirty skin bloomed red. Morin's lips went white as she pressed them shut, refusing to give her captors the satisfaction of acknowledging her pain.

"I'm angry at everyone involved in the site," Petra pointed out. "I might go so far as to call myself steamed."

She was feigning bravery, but Morin's eyes dilated as the kettle tilted on its side. Petra was playing for keeps today.

Petra yanked the kettle away and huffed as the boiling water trickled over the waiting tea bags.

"He promised Dark Hound was a game!" Fear rasped her voice.

Norah checked in with the tangle of oozing emotions. *Shame. She's ashamed.*

"You didn't believe him, though," Norah guessed.

Morin blinked hard, eyes watering. Petra refilled the kettle and replaced it on the stove, muttering, "You can never have too much tea," with a pointed look at Morin's bare ankles.

Lincoln cleared his throat. "I've got the site up." A glowing three-dimensional image of a pixie rose out of his phone screen.

"Do you *wish* you could wield a longer wand?" a syrupy voice chirped. The pixie pulled a holographic wand from the phone, and it doubled over on itself like a licorice whip. "Uh-oh! Don't let this happen to you. Stumps are for chumps. Loopy's Lathe Lacquer can help."

"Did you click on another popup ad?" Norah asked.

"The screen is so damn small," Lincoln muttered, snatching the holographic pixie and stuffing it back down. After three more clicks, the crimson Dark Hound grid appeared. Petra, eyes sliding over the image of her face, commandeered the phone and dropped it not very gently on Morin's chest. Retrieving her wand, Petra pointed at a starburst in a corner.

"That's Celsiora Maple. I officiated her wedding. She

threatened to steal the ceremony for her daughter's wedding, but she didn't make it."

Fierce sorrow whirled into a ball above Morin's chest. Norah nodded encouragingly at her mother.

Petra pointed at another face. "That's Vanya. I never did learn his last name since we were under deep cover. We spent a week staking out this creepy dwarf, and he hardly said more than four words to me the whole time. He had the most amazing talent for whistling.

"On the last day of the stakeout, I blew our cover by getting coffee. Our mark sent a murder of mechanical crows after us. I was badly injured, but Vanya took them all out with delicately placed throwing darts. He whistled Dvořák's *Cello Concerto* to me until a witch who wasn't drained from battling the clockwork menagerie showed up to heal me.

"I once saw Yo-Yo Ma perform that piece at the Hollywood Bowl, and I prefer it whistled. That was Vanya."

A tear streamed down Morin's face, and Petra tapped another head. "That's Claudette. Her widow never knew she was a witch and still hopes she's alive. Miguel... Okay, to be honest, he was an asshole. I think he only joined for the battle magic training. He had a tiny dog he brought on all the missions that was as mean as he was. A pair of obnoxious pricks. But the dog pulled a whole litter of stunned cat shifters out of a drainpipe once. I thought they were going to be lunch, but the dog dropped them on dry land and growled until they woke up."

The look on Morin's face suggested she might have preferred the boiling sponge bath.

Petra went through the names of the dead witches and

wizards one by one. Morin was drained, her emotions a dark mist.

"I didn't kill anyone," she said, though her certainty wavered. "It's not my fault. What's next? You going to try Vladimir Putin's webmaster for war crimes?"

"Let me do some reading on human rights cyberlaw and get back to you," Lincoln said.

"I try to set my ethical standards a little higher than Putin's IT guy," Petra growled.

Norah leaned in. "I know you didn't want to kill anyone." Morin's emotions pulsed with faint acknowledgment. "That's good. Help us take down the site. You can save the other witches and wizards." She pointed at the grid. Petra rolled her eyes and gazed longingly at the whistling teapot. After a moment of hesitation, she sighed and turned the burner off.

"I used to be a programmer," Morin finally said. "The classic setup. An office full of ping-pong tables and kegs I never had time to enjoy because I was always hunched over, pecking away at the latest backend crisis. Plus, half my subordinates treated me like their mommy. I had to teach two separate men how to make a dentist's appointment. In their thirties. Pathetic. They'd shit on my code in meetings, then expect me to comfort them when they were dumped."

"For someone fishing for sympathy, you sure have abetted a lot of murders," Petra muttered.

Morin scowled. "The tech company I was at had this beautiful indoor garden. Someone published a paper about how access to nature increases productivity, so boom...we got a garden. I was in the office at two AM for the third time that week. I had a camping cot there.

"The CEO fucking loved it. He called me Jane Goodall, sleeping in the field with my code monkeys. My arms were giving me trouble, so I went to the garden, and I had a total mental breakdown. I cried into a philodendron for an hour. The soil was so sweet and loamy that I put my hands in it. Just buried them in it. What incredibly friable earth it was. My fingers felt better. I emailed my boss my resignation letter the next morning."

As she spoke, her eyes slid to a bushy plant flourishing in the kitchen window. She turned quickly away, but not before a thread of affection shot toward the wide leaves. Philodendrons had wide leaves.

"I sold my place in San Francisco and spent every cent I had on this land, but you need more than land. You need tools, and annual seed loans, and a fucking Instagram page. My buddy loaned me some money. An old friend. When he asked me to do some magically-enhanced coding, I couldn't say no."

"Who's the friend?" Norah asked. Morin pressed her lips shut again and shook her head. Fear twisted out of her. Although she was still stunned, she shivered.

"Who's the friend?" Norah repeated louder. Carlisle, a bird shifter she repped, had auditioned for a Mafia movie recently. She tried to imitate the threatening line he'd read.

Unfortunately, Morin was more afraid of her friend than she was of Norah and kept her mouth shut. Norah stood and sauntered over to the kettle on the stove.

"If you think *you* can hurt me, imagine what someone

with an IQ of 215 and no moral compass can do," Morin stuttered.

"You need nicer friends," Petra remarked between sips of tea.

Norah hefted the teapot.

"Oh, this isn't for you." Stretching across the counter, she lifted the spout above the roots of the philodendron in the kitchen window. The panic that hit Norah in response was so intense that, for a moment, she thought it had come from the plant.

"No! Don't hurt Lodi!" Morin screamed.

"Tech people," Lincoln muttered disapprovingly.

Morin loved this plant more than she loved her alligator. Norah was mystified but let a tiny drizzle of boiling water hiss into the soil.

"Tell me, or the plant gets it. You think your vegetables will respect you when you can't keep your prize philodendron alive?"

"Please!" Morin cried.

"You have five seconds before Lodi becomes creamed spinach." Norah lifted the teapot higher.

Morin choked, and she thought she might have to follow through. A moment later, the fight went out of Morin's eyes.

"His name is Cook Forester. He's a tech entrepreneur. He started a dating website called Humpr."

"'Humpr?' Really?" Norah asked. Four years ago, she'd gone on an online dating spree. She'd met exactly one person from Humpr, who'd asked her for her measurements in the first ten minutes of the date. When she'd said she didn't know and tried to laugh it off, he'd pulled out a tape.

"What's Humpr?" Petra asked.

"It's a dating website. Uses a fancy algorithm to generate bad decisions. I'd call it a cesspit."

Norah's mother raised a silent eyebrow, and her father suffered a sudden-onset coughing fit.

"Cook Forester runs Dark Hound?"

"He's who I report to when I work on it. And..."

"What?" Norah waved the kettle menacingly at the philodendron.

"He's the one who bought all the impfruit," Morin said. "I thought he was playing a prank on his CTO. They do that shit all the time."

"Do you know where Dark Hound is hosted?" Norah asked.

Morin shook her head. "Cook has a big office complex in Santa Monica. If you could get in, you might be able to figure out who's actually running the show."

"I thought you were old tech buddies? You're his green-grocer, too?"

"Yeah. It's a thank you for the loan. A couple times a month, I take big shipments of produce to him. He used to come to the farm, but he's been super busy lately."

"When's the next delivery?" Norah asked, a bright idea germinating.

"In two days. Why?"

"Lucky for you, you have a few new delivery drivers."

CHAPTER SIXTEEN

"Vesta, water my plants," Norah said. Thunder rumbled softly near the ceiling as her magical assistant floated placidly into the air. Small clouds appeared above the houseplants in Norah's living room, emitting a pleasant patter of rain. With early morning light slanting through the windows, the effect was idyllic.

In a vase in the living room window, the cantankerose jerked to its full height. "What the fuck? I was napping!"

Norah shushed him. Lodi the philodendron, whom she had taken as a hostage, was not thriving in its new environment. Pepe had treated the plant as his personal salad bar until Norah lectured him on maintaining bargaining power.

"You're gonna be okay, bud," she told the plant, guiltily eyeing a half-chewed leaf near its base. "Don't you want to have fun with your new friends?" she asked the collection of wan green leaves, gesturing at the Oriceran plants, which sparkled with light along their veins.

"*L is for the way your leaves are green*," she sang softly. "*O is oxygen you maaaake for meeee...*"

A huff from the cantankerose was not drowned out by the small cloud over its head. "Oh, yeah, sure. Like that stray-cat screeching is going to turn things around for Sadboy McWilty here." Norah shot blue magic into the cloud over the rose's head, and the resulting flood shut him up.

Her Oriceran aloe swayed under the misting from its small cloud, joined by Norah's other plants.

"How come you never sang for me?" a voice from the kitchen doorway asked. Norah reached for her wand, only to drop her hand back to her side with a grin when she saw the hovering six-sided figure.

"Cleo!" Norah squealed and ran over to embrace the flying wooden crate. The cursed pixie seemed the same, though her winged Hermes sneakers were caked with fine black dirt.

"I've missed you."

"Hmmm, likely story," Cleo said. "Pepe let me in. I see he's already replaced me in your affections." As she spoke, the runes carved into her side glowed, and she kicked the corner of Pepe's half-eaten luxury dog bed.

The lock on the front door clicked open. Norah dove for her wand again, then relaxed at the sound of hoofbeats in the hall. The tuft of white hair on Pepe's chin waggled as he poked his head in.

"Welcome home," Norah muttered, eyeing the housekey gripped between the goat's lips. It was attached to a fetching pink velvet ribbon wound around his black-and-white ruff. When he spat out the key, a drop of drool landed on Norah's shoe.

"I pay rent here," Norah muttered. "It's not a boarding house."

"Oh, please. I lived here for years. I could probably claim squatter's rights. And Pepe knows me," Cleo added. Norah was once again amazed by the cube's ability to shrug.

"What brings you home?"

Cleo glowed brightly. "I got a job as a camera operator!"

Norah glanced at Cleo's wooden feet and raised an eyebrow. Cleo flew over and kicked her in the arm.

"Don't give me that look. It's a remote-control system. I'm like a drone, but with better reaction speeds and more artistry. I spent last weekend filming a paper airplane competition for the Discovery Channel."

"Huh!"

Pepe snorted encouragingly.

"I think I have a talent for cinematography," Cleo continued. "Back when I was acting, it was all gruff old farts who spent all their time in darkrooms. I might take a UCLA extension class. Apply for an aide to do the button-pushing."

The conversation stuck in Norah's mind as she drove to the office. Around eleven, Madge poked her in the nose, carrying her toothpick-sized wand. "What's going on? You've been distracted all day."

Norah looked up from Frondle's *Green & Pointy*

contract, which she'd run her eyes over five or six times without taking in a single word.

"I want to get Cleo those hands." Norah relayed the pixie's newfound passion for cinematography.

"I know you want to play nice, but I'm still willing to go full St. George on that wooden dragon's ass."

Norah thought about the glint in the living marionette's eyes and snorted. "Tempting, but I'd rather track down fresh brainwood, or at least try. I can only handle pissing off so many puppeteers."

"I get it. You don't want to wind up in a basement with a hand up your ass," Madge rasped, eyeing Norah quizzically. After a moment, an ostentatious sigh dropped the pixie half a foot in the air.

"What is it?"

"Nothing." Madge scooped a pen cap of coffee from the pot and alighted on the edge of the counter to drink it. Norah glared until she finished and continued, "Outside of the go-go boys at Long Wands, you only have one real option for accessing high-quality wood."

Norah knew who Madge was talking about. "No. I don't trust him."

"Talk to Angelo," Madge insisted. "See what he says."

"Who's Angelo, your boyfriend? Sounds like a jerk," a gruff voice said from behind Norah's computer. She'd brought the cantankerose to work with her, afraid that if she left it at home, Pepe would eat it. She wasn't sure the little goat would win that battle.

Madge lofted over and kicked the crimson petals with one pointy shoe.

"What would you know, you old fart?" she asked. "You couldn't pollinate a pistil with a fire hydrant."

"You haven't gotten laid in so long, your wand isn't the only thing covered in pixie dust," the cantankerose sneered.

Norah stared winsomely at Sweetie's spangled horns inside the orb of the snow globe on her desk. *This place could use some positive energy.*

"Fine. I'll talk to Angelo." She poked the cantankerose in the middle of its bud. "If you insult any of my clients, I'll make you an edible arrangement if I have to eat you myself."

"Go ahead. I'm rich in vitamin C, you—" The slamming door cut off the gruff voice.

She purchased a small bottle of kimchi ranch from the pizza place downstairs before making the drive to Burbank. She realized she hadn't heard from Angelo since they'd gone to the farmers' market together. No obsequious texts, no gift baskets, only silence. That was what she'd wanted, so why was she nervous?

The commercial kitchen was overseen by a familiar and extremely harried young chef, the soup witch. On Norah's last visit, the place had been an extra virgin olive-oiled machine. Today it was a war zone. She watched with raised eyebrows as two chefs threw a fire blanket over a stockpot full of licking acid-green flames.

Panting, they put their heads together before the soup witch broke off toward Norah.

"Soup girl!" Norah called.

"My name is Zeynab, and I'm twenty-eight."

Norah felt guilty. "My apologies, Chef."

"We're busy. What do you want?" Zeynab asked.

Norah pointed out that a green flame was climbing the young chef's sleeve.

"Shit." The woman plunged her arm into a nearby bowl of cream. It sizzled, and a wizard returning from the walk-in freezers at the back of the kitchen cursed.

"I've been steeping that for forty-five minutes!"

Zeynab cringed. "I was on fire."

He glared, but then his eyes registered the small jar in Norah's hands. "Ooh! Kimchi ranch!" He snatched it from her and raced to contain some oncoming crisis.

"I don't want to interrupt you," Norah confessed to Zeynab. "But I need to talk to Angelo."

The chef gawked as if she were a space alien. "Angelo's not *here*." She swept her hand over the chaotic room as if that explained everything.

"Do you know where he went?"

"If I knew where he *was*," Zeynab told her, "I would be there with an immersion blender, pureeing his guts for leaving me in the fucking lurch. Now, put on an apron and help, or get out of my kitchen."

Norah fled before the overbearing chef could press her into service. Staring at the chaos from the sidewalk outside, she dialed Angelo's number. It went immediately to a message saying his voicemail was full. Duncan hadn't seen him either, as it turned out.

Norah's stomach sank in a way that had little to do with the quantity of kimchi ranch she'd eaten in the past twenty-four hours. Would Domenico move against his own son? He hadn't played nice with anyone else.

There was a small explosion inside the window, and a

harried voice screamed, "That's not water! That's overproof rum, idiot!"

It was time to put a few miles between her and this epicenter of culinary disaster.

There was one more person who might be able to find brainwood. Reluctantly, Norah turned her car toward the cemetery.

Neither the peacocks nor the stray cats were visible among the cool gray headstones. Hopefully, this was détente, not a symptom of mutual annihilation.

The mausoleum sat alone on its island under the misty flat light of the afternoon.

The stairs to Stellan's workshop were dark and steep today. Norah's steps fell heavily on the stone in the long hallway, and the enormous granite jaws at the entrance to the workshop seemed less like festive decorations than an active threat. The pear-shaped ruby dangling from one of the fangs scintillated as it swayed, and Norah's pace slowed. When she was three feet away, a geological noise boomed, and the jaws of the entryway snapped shut. Fine grains of crushed stone clattered against Norah's boots. With its mouth closed, the colossal stone face was a cross between a heavy-jawed dog and a devil, its eyes closed as if it were sleeping. It was so lifelike that Norah reached to check if it was stone.

"I wouldn't do that," a voice above Norah rasped.

The monstrous hound's right eye opened with a slow scrape. Inside was not an eyeball, but another face, a cheeky gargoyle carved from the same sleek granite. It stuck its tongue out at Norah and crossed its eyes.

"Uh, hey! Eyeball monster."

The gargoyle glowered at her. "Stellan wants to know if you're still repping that evil puppeteer."

Norah nodded. The enormous eyelid snapped closed, and muffled voices conferred beyond the stone face.

The eyelid opened with a snap. The gargoyle sucked in its lips and hocked a pebble at Norah's feet. She sidestepped, and it rolled past her down the dark corridor.

"Stellan's enemies are not welcome in his domain," the gargoyle stated formally. "That means beat it, witch."

"It's for Cleo," Norah added.

The eyelid slammed shut again, and the low chatter resumed. A second later, it opened again.

"Stellan says Cleo is welcome to ask for his help directly," the gargoyle grumbled. "Look, lady, have you heard of the internet? I can be equally unhelpful in email, and you could save yourself a lot of time."

"I need to know where Stellan gets his wood."

The gargoyle sighed, looking very put out at having to do its job.

When it reappeared, it rolled its eyes. "He's not giving you his lumber guy's name, but if you find any two-by-fours, he has some recommendations about where to put them." This was delivered with slightly less bravado, and the eyelid slammed shut. This time, it failed to reopen.

Just as Norah was about to knock again, there was a hiss, and steam blasted from the dog devil's slitted stone nose. Norah pulled back her hand before she was scalded.

"That's your plan, Stellan? Burn me alive? Very mature!"

The steam outflow increased. She could contain it with magic, but if she forced her way into the workshop to an uncertain outcome, she would have to face angry goths with construction tools. Sighing, she jogged away from the roiling steam.

If Stellan wouldn't give her a name, she would have to take it. Back in the car, she dialed a number. Uriel picked up almost before she finished dialing.

"What?"

"I need you to hack into someone's records."

"Ugh! No more calendars. I'll die of boredom."

"This is much more interesting," Norah lied. "I need you to see where Stellan buys his lumber. The business name is Stellan's Cellar."

"Hm."

"His system is magically protected," Norah added, trying to make it sound like an enticing challenge. It was probably true.

"Fine, but I want two pizzas this time. Whenever you ask for a boring favor, I'm doubling the number of bribery pizzas."

"Mr. Kim will be thrilled," Norah said.

CHAPTER SEVENTEEN

U riel wanted his payment up front, so Norah dropped by Kim's Pizza on her way back to the office.

"What's your weirdest pizza?" she asked.

Ji-woo brushed his silky hair behind one ear. "Weird is in the eye of the beholder, but we don't get too many orders for the banchan."

"What's on that?"

"Soy-braised lotus root and jeotgal."

"What's jeotgal?"

"Technically it's any kind of salted seafood, but ours is made with pickled pollack intestine."

Pickled pollack intestine. Was it as much of a mouthful to eat as it was to say? "Is it good?" Norah asked skeptically.

Ji-woo raised an eyebrow. "Is caviar good?"

"Hmmm. Fine. I'll take two banchan pizzas."

"Two? Have you considered, you know, starting small?"

Norah shook her head.

Fifteen minutes later, two boxes emitting unusual, intensely savory aromas appeared.

"Can I get extra kimchi ranch?" she asked.

"That's cheating," Ji-woo said. "You can't appreciate new flavors if you drown them."

After a moment, he relented. Norah carried the collection up to the roof and deposited it next to Uriel, who had built himself an awning and covered the roof beneath it in woven rugs. The makeshift space looked nicer than Norah's office.

"Two pizzas, per your demand." She plunked them in front of him.

Uriel sniffed the air. "Is that sausage?"

"No. What's the address?"

The coder peeked under the lid of the box and pulled a lacy brown lotus root off the top of the pizza.

"That's not pepperoni." He nibbled it.

"A deal's a deal. Now, where is the lumberyard?"

Uriel's eyes widened as he swallowed the lotus root. "That's phenomenal." He grabbed the largest piece of pizza from the box and tucked into it with small but enthusiastic bites.

Norah had never seen a face so rapt, and she'd been to two different meditation retreats in Big Sur. Frowning, she poked open the box and grabbed the smallest sliver.

"Oh, my God!" she exclaimed as the mélange of flavors hit her tongue.

"I've wasted my life on pepperoni," Uriel proclaimed.

Norah chewed with great relish. Fish innards. Who knew? The kimchi ranch lay forgotten in its plastic bag.

When she reached for another piece, Uriel slammed the cardboard shut before her hand weaseled in.

"We agreed on two pizzas." He glared at the grease under her fingernails. "Not one and seven-eighths."

"Round up," Norah muttered. "Now. The address?"

Uriel's computer screen flashed through a series of rapid images. Had he gotten faster at typing in the past week? "Downtown," he finally stated. "I'm airdropping you the location."

As Norah headed to her car, she resisted the urge to buy five or six more banchan pizzas for the ride.

The warehouse district was full of looming buildings and dotted with lonely cafes, food trucks, and galleries. The place was in mid-revitalization, and the address Uriel directed Norah to resembled an art studio, not a lumber yard. Two wormy pigeons fought over a smear of food on the sidewalk outside. An icy man greeted her at a small desk by the door. He was either extremely young and stoic, or he'd gotten a lot of Botox.

"I'm looking for..." Norah glanced at her phone. "Knut?"

"Do you have an appointment?" the receptionist asked, picking a speck of dirt out from under one orange-painted fingernail.

"Uh, Stellan sent me?" Norah asked. This produced actual interest, and she was waved into the enormous open space. Home improvement was a mystery to Norah, but the long boards piled into rows of metal shelves appeared to be valuable. A saw buzzed in the distance, and the place smelled phenomenal. Norah's wand shivered in her pocket as they passed a neat pile of blue eucalyptus boards.

"Aw, hey!" Norah pulled it out. "It's your family." The wand vibrated.

"Can I help you?" a dry voice asked. The figure who emerged from the shadows in the distance looked like nothing Norah had ever seen before. He was taller than Frondle. More peculiarly, he was made of wood.

"You're made of wood," Norah said dumbly.

Leaves rustled as the figure shook its head. "I'm not *made* of wood. I *am* wood." Twiggy fingers spindled out from a central trunk, and bulbous branches grew in a crown around his head. Instead of legs, a collection of tentacled roots moved him across the ocean of concrete with a bobbing, spidery motion. His eyes were knots, and his mouth was a gaping owl hole.

"You're a dryad," Norah stated. They were rare on Earth and rarer still in the urban sea of Los Angeles. "*You're* the lumber guy?"

Wood creaked as the dryad went still.

"I'm Knut Barkley. Is that a problem?" There was a tense note in the voice now, like a board under stress.

"You're a dryad. Isn't it...uncomfortable to sell wood?"

"People are made of meat, and they work as butchers." The dryad sounded both offended and slightly rehearsed. "I don't like you."

Nice going, Wintry. "I'm sorry. You're not doing anything wrong."

"I know I'm not. Who said I was doing anything wrong? I think you should leave."

Knut raised an arm-branch, and a thin spear of wood grew toward her, leaves rustling as it lodged in her shoulder. The branch retreated, and Norah winced. *I deserved that.*

She tugged the splinter from her skin, wiping away a drop of welling blood.

"I need to ask you a few...owww!" She yelped as needles of pain shot through her left arm. Had the dryad barraged her with more splinters? No, her arms were as smooth as ever. The pain receded as she rubbed the spot, and she took a breath. "Can you answer a few...ahhh."

The burning needles appeared between her shoulder blades. It was much harder to reach this one. She vowed to do more yoga.

There was something unnatural about the sensation.

"What did you do to me? Ouch!" More prickles stabbed into the tops of her feet. It was like having aggressive acupuncture done with upholstery needles.

"I don't like you," the dryad added. "I also know Stellan didn't send you, so I put a curse on you."

The pain subsided enough for Norah to speak.

"What did you—" The instant the words left her mouth, the burning discomfort roared back to life.

"An excellent cure for loquacious intruders. Every time you say a word, you get a splinter. When you go away? No splinters. Heal thyself, loser."

"How dare you!" Each of her words was punctuated by a sharp prick.

"I'm not doing anything," the dryad pointed out. "You're doing it to yourself."

It was a nice piece of magic. Annoying, but she could imagine scenarios where she wouldn't mind using a similar curse. Like, for instance, on her Humpr match, who had spent their date monologuing about 1950s German cinema.

"C'mon, ask me anything you want. It'll be fun!" The dryad's trunk leaned expectantly forward, and his mouth opened slightly.

Norah took a deep breath. Time to be strategic. "I need brainwood," she said. Four pricks of pain danced across her collarbone. "Hey, no fair. Brainwood is one wor... Ow! Fuck!" *I swear to God, tree, I am going to turn you into a birdhouse and give you to the most diseased pigeon I can find.*

"Brainwood? That's an interesting request. What do you need brainwood for? Please describe your plans in extensive detail."

Norah glowered, choosing her words carefully. "Marionette hands. For box friend." Five points of pain shot through her scalp. This splinter curse was getting old fast.

"What on the Green Man's earth is a 'box friend?'" the dryad asked, looking genuinely interested.

Norah gritted her teeth and steeled herself. "Former pixie. Cursed. Now box. Needs hands for cinematography."

"That's quite the mouthful."

"She's also wood." The next stabs appeared in the small of her back. The pain was exceeding her limits.

She pulled her wand out without a real plan. Knut smirked. "Hello there, twig."

The wand shivered.

"Hey!" Norah winced. *Fuck it.* She raised her arm and shot a stunning spell at Knut. Or she tried to. Nothing happened, though her wand vibrated. It was like getting a magical error message.

Norah shook the blue gum eucalyptus hard. "Traitor.

Good luck getting oiled after this." The wood shivered under her glare.

"That's no way to treat a friend," the dryad said. "Hmmm. How about I trade you? Your box friend's number for the brainwood lead. She sounds very interesting."

It was difficult for a tree to look lascivious, but Knut pulled it off. Norah kept her eyeline well above any bulging knots in the lower trunk. An idea sparking in her mind, and she grinned.

"Piece of paper?" she asked, grimacing with pain.

Knut rolled his eyes. "Bring me my tablet, Topher," he shouted. The young receptionist appeared moments later with a tablet and stylus. Knut turned back to Norah. "Paper's creepy, even for me. It's not as though *you* go around writing notes to yourself on ground beef."

He had a point. Norah wrote a number on the tablet. Seeing it, the dryad's gaping knot of a mouth twisted.

"That wasn't so hard, was it? Now, the brainwood. There's a stand of it in Topanga Canyon, planted by a botanist who got sucked into Oriceran in the seventies. Everyone thought he'd taken too many psychedelics. He filled his pockets with seeds and found an out-of-the-way place in the state park to plant them."

Norah thought for a minute. "Coordinates?" This time, the pain stabbed her cheek below her eye.

Knut shook his head. Norah half-jumped as the motion startled a small bird out of a nest on his shoulder.

"Let's see how the first date with your box goes." He tapped a wooden finger on the tablet.

Shit. Topanga State Park was a big place, but now she had somewhere to start.

"Don't worry. You'll only feel the curse when you're within a hundred feet of me. Bye-bye, now. Don't let a two-by-four hit you on the way out!"

Once she was a safe distance from the warehouse, she tested a tentative word. "Shit?" Nothing happened.

Norah sighed in relief and called Madge. The pixie picked up immediately.

"You'll never believe who I met."

When she had finished relaying the story, Madge went silent.

"What?" Norah asked.

"Nothing. I can't believe you gave that creep Cleo's number."

"Oh. I didn't."

"Whose number did you give him?" Madge asked.

Norah hesitated. "Hazel's. I assumed a fire elemental could deal with a creepy tree."

Madge snorted. "I guess we're not getting more granular directions than an entire state park, then."

"No," Norah agreed. Not for the first time, she felt extremely lucky to have the allies she did.

CHAPTER EIGHTEEN

Norah's new backpack, which she'd purchased from a ritzy local equipment store, was ninety percent straps. She fished through them to find a place to stash her water bottle. Cleo lolled on the sofa as Madge secured a tiny leather fanny pack around her waist. It had taken Norah a week to put together the expedition.

"I can't believe you made me buy *hiking* gear. I had to talk to a wrinkly fairy with tatted-up bat wings about backpacking in Joshua Tree for *an hour*. Do you know where the best backcountry camping sites are, Norah?"

"No."

Madge's eyes compressed into slits. "Well, to my dismay, *I* do. Like I'd spend my leisure time in the forest. That's where owls live. Freaky-ass neck-rotating feather faces. The fairy tried to sell me boots, too, like I'd be Oregon Trailing my way across the goddamn dirt. Pixies have wings for a reason, you know."

She stroked the new leather. "It *is* nice work, I guess. I think it's made of..." She scrutinized the living room, reconnoitering the undersides of the plant tables, then dropped her voice to a whisper. *"Goat leather."*

A hoof stamped sharply on the terracotta tile, and Pepe trotted into the living room with a murderous look in his eye and a water bottle between his teeth. Under his icy glare, Madge flew up and perched on the edge of a hanging plant. "You're not exactly Smoky the Bear."

Madge eyed Norah's purple spandex leggings and matching crop top and mesh windbreaker. "Don't holes defeat the purpose of a coat?" She poked her toothpick wand through the black netting.

"Hey! I was a junior ranger!" Norah protested.

"Did that involve extensive training?" Madge asked.

"I don't remember. I was seven. Anyway, you're one to talk. What are *you* wearing?"

Madge twirled so cheerfully that she shed glowing dust. The pixie was wearing a neon-yellow tracksuit printed with a mix of plaid and tiny cats. Floral embroidery took it so far over the top that it was cool. "Hey! I'm a Hollywood mover and shaker. I need something comfortable to move and shake in."

Pepe snorted, and Norah glared at him. "Are you sure you want to come?"

The goat rolled his eyes and sat on his haunches by the door. Unfortunately, his rest was interrupted when the door was slammed open. He was sent flying across the tile. He bleated in annoyance, and his water bottle rolled across the floor.

Quint burst in. The dinner-plate-sized sunglasses that covered half his face could not disguise his haggard expression. He slurped a cold brew and raged at Norah. "You!"

"Hey, Quint! Nice to see you. Please tell me you're not hiking with us." She leaned toward Madge and added in an undertone, "He goes twice as fast as everyone else, then does jumping jacks until we catch up. It's annoying."

Madge made a gratifyingly disgusted noise.

"Hazel and I had coffee for the first time in months. It was going well. You know, the old back-and-forth banter like it was at the start. Then I asked her to get drinks with me this weekend, and you know what she said?"

"I'd rather poke my eyes out with one of your little jam spoons?" Norah guessed.

"I'd rather choke on a keto muffin?" Madge interjected, swinging her legs.

Cleo took off from the couch, runes glowing with amusement. "I would rather be crushed by a kettlebell?"

Quint glared at each in turn. "She said she met someone. She said *you* introduced them." His lengthy sip of cold brew produced extended unpleasant slurping noises. "He's kind of goth but really into nature."

"What happened to Glesselda?" Cleo finally asked, glancing at the crystal coffin in which the light elf's son was frozen.

"The last time we hung out, she wanted to use me as a footstool. I'm not a footstool, Cleo! I'm a human being!"

"That's debatable," Norah muttered. "Wait, are you talking about Knut?"

"Who's Knut?" Quint asked.

"I, uh... Don't worry about it."

Norah's eyebrows stayed up, and Madge pressed her face into a leaf to stop herself from laughing. Knut and

Hazel had hit it off? Norah could smell the *Romeo and Juliet* remake.

Quint flung himself onto the sofa. "I was so close, and he snatched her away."

Cleo made a lazy circle around the room, then swooped in and kicked Quint in the back of the head.

"Ow!"

"Hazel's not a piece of furniture either, you know," Cleo countered. "She can't be *taken*."

"I would enjoy seeing someone try," Norah said. Pepe bleated in agreement.

"Don't think of her as being stolen from you. Think of her as running away from you with great rapidity," Madge pointed out.

Quint grumbled, slurped, and stared at his empty cup. "I need more coffee."

"Then go back to work," Norah said. "We're going hiking."

Quint flung his empty coffee cup at her. It landed a foot short and rolled across the tile to Pepe, who took an enthusiastic bite and made a noise that sounded like "Thanks." Norah stared at the black-and-white goat as Quint stormed away.

"Ugh. Quint should have gone into prestige television," Norah muttered when he was out of earshot.

"Why?"

"Because he loooooovvves drama."

She held her hand up for a high-five, and Cleo hit it with the sole of her foot at the apex of an elegant somersault.

When Norah told Cleo about the brainwood and the

hands, she'd been worried. She didn't want Cleo to think she was overstepping. However, the pixie had been enthusiastic about the idea and had insisted on coming along.

They spent an engaging forty-five minutes on the drive to Topanga making fun of her brother. Norah hoped things with Glesselda had ended amicably. She didn't want a near-omnipotent light elf as an enemy…or an in-law.

They paid their ten bucks at the ranger station, and Norah reluctantly fished through her backpack's many straps for the ones that went over her shoulder. As she looked into the shadows between the trees, she had no idea what to do now. There was a tug on the straps as Madge landed on Norah's pack.

"Lead the way." Apparently, the pixie didn't intend to exert herself, brand-new goat-leather fanny pack or not.

Norah paused at the trailhead to orient herself, unfolding the topographical map she'd purchased for the expedition. She pointed at the forest's perimeter.

"If there's a hidden experimental forest, it's probably away from the trail, which means I need aerial surveillance. You're going to have to fly." She jabbed her backpack with a finger, and Madge yelped. After a moment, grudging pixie-wing flapping reached her ear.

"Let's cover the eastern edge of the park for now," Norah suggested. "We might not get this done in one day. I want you flanking me, Madge to my left, and Cleo to my right. Meet up every thirty minutes or so, and we'll mark off the ground we covered."

Madge shouted at Norah as she began a looping ascent, "You owe me a massage after this. A lion tamarin shifter I know does amazing work, and he's not cheap."

With that, she was gone. Norah trudged up the trail, Pepe clopping behind.

After less than an hour, she wished she'd brought Quint. Pepe was a competent hiker, but he wasn't much of a conversationalist. Every few minutes, he stopped and sniffed the air, staring keenly into the forest.

"You're not secretly a bloodhound in disguise, are you?" Norah asked. Pepe shook his head.

"You understand me?"

"Baaaaaaa."

"Are you really a goat?"

Pepe stood still for a moment, then trotted up the trail with a flick of his tail. Whatever the maybe-a-goat's deal was, he would reveal it in his own sweet time.

At their next stop, Madge flung herself across the leaves of a rabbit's ear plant. Cleo leaned against a log, runes glowing more faintly than usual.

"What have you seen?" Norah asked.

"Trees," Madge grumbled.

"What kind of trees?"

"I don't know. Green ones. Do I look like a forest nymph to you?"

"Okay, fine. Have you seen anything…not of this earth?"

"No," Cleo said. Madge shook her head.

Norah spread the topo map across the log and marked off the areas they'd searched. They had only been out for two hours, and she'd drunk three-quarters of her water. The pace was fine, but the temperature was pushing ninety, and it was unseasonably humid.

The break stretched for longer than was strictly necessary until Pepe, appointing himself the taskmaster, kicked them increasingly less gently until they hauled themselves up and continued down the trail.

The temperatures cooled in the early evening. Norah glanced skeptically at the sun, which was sinking below a nearby hilltop.

"I guess we should head home. We're about a mile from the trailhead." Norah spent an exhausted minute trying to re-fold the topographic map before crumpling it into a ball and stomping it with a foot until it was small enough to fit into her pack.

When they hadn't reached their car in half an hour, Norah assumed they were dragging more than she realized. When they hadn't reached it in an hour, she flung her pack next to the trail and put her head in her hands. With the sun behind the mountains, it had gotten dark fast.

"I think we're lost." Something howled in the forest, and the white stripe of hair across Pepe's back stood up. He growled in a very un-goat-like way in the direction of the noise.

Madge plopped next to Norah and poked her in the thigh with her tiny wand. "Hey! No moping. We're not defenseless fawns. We're strong independent women with magical powers." Pepe bleated in protest. "Plus whatever Pepe is," Madge amended.

"I don't know if I'm up for living off the land," Norah told her wanly. "Can one of you take a look? Maybe there's a light on at the ranger station that you can see from the sky."

Cleo glowed in agreement and took off, frightening a few bats as she wound her way above the trees. She disappeared until suddenly, her runes blazed brighter than the surrounding stars.

"I hope she sees something."

The glowing cube dove, whooping enthusiastically. A few feet above the trees, she shouted excitedly, "Guys, I saw a—"

A dark shape whistling through the trees cut her off. A net swooped around Cleo and dragged her away, screaming.

Pepe galloped into the trees before Norah could stop him. She summoned a ball of light, following Cleo's voice off-trail. The ground was thick with vegetation, and she summoned a spinning blue blade to chop through the undergrowth, shooting a silent apology to the State Park Service as she did. *Some junior ranger I am.*

For a minute, Cleo's shouts got closer, then they faded. Norah picked up her pace. "Where is she?"

Oh, wait, I have built-in emotional radar.

She reached inside and turned the magic on. Madge was a clear bright burst of energy in the trees ahead of her. Farther ahead, Cleo was disoriented. Pepe was a furious red ball moving away from her at a speed closer to that of a sports car than a goat.

There was another person, too—the one who had kidnapped Cleo. Their emotions were cautious and protective, more a mama bear than rampaging bull. Norah locked onto the signal and pushed her pace until, at last, the edge of her magical blue light brushed a dark moving figure up ahead.

"Cleo!" Norah shouted. A muffled noise reached her ears as her magical sense picked up a current of relief.

The moving figure executed an astonishing vault into the branches of a large oak tree ahead. The outline of a dark teardrop was visible against the glow of the night sky. The figure struggling inside was almost certainly Cleo.

Norah slowed her steps as the forest spat her into a clearing bright with moonlight, the buttery yellow glow illuminating a rustic campsite.

Wait. That's not moonlight.

It was sunlight. Past the oak, pear-shaped sunfruit glowed on a small but heavily-laden tree. This must have been what Cleo had seen from the sky.

Pepe charged into the clearing and struck the base of the oak with both hooves. Norah wouldn't have put tree-climbing past him, but he stayed on the ground.

"There's a razor arrow pointed at your heart," a low voice growled. "Razor arrows aren't made. They're grown. Their points are an atom thick, and they can pierce dwarven armor. I wouldn't recommend coming any closer."

Norah stilled.

"There's no way he can see well enough to hit me," Madge whispered.

"I can see the uneven stitching on your astonishingly ugly garment," the voice snarled.

There was a small, sharp intake of breath from the air above Norah's head. "Hey! This is Gucci!"

A dark silhouette dropped from a branch and stepped

into Norah's blue magical light. A wood elf. Both of his large eyes had two irises, which wandered restlessly across the whites. He was short, and he hadn't bothered camouflaging himself. Had he been expecting company?

Wiry arm muscles effortlessly pulled back the string of a sleek compound bow. The weapon was stunning, carved from ebony and polished to a starlight-reflecting shine. A distinctly cubic shape struggled in the woven hemp net hanging from the wood elf's shoulder.

"Refrain from kicking me, or I will shoot your friends," the wood elf muttered. The cube collapsed into the bottom of the sack. "I thought I knew every kind of plant, but I've never seen anything like your friend here."

"I'm a bona fide original!" Cleo's voice was muffled by the enveloping fabric.

"So you are." The muscles holding the bowstring taut relaxed infinitesimally. "I'm Yolen."

"I'm Norah. This is Madge, and the pixie in your bag is Cleo."

His eyebrows shot up. "Pixie? I am not stupid. I know what pixies look like." The arrow tip homed in on Norah's unprotected chest. Her mesh windbreaker had been a poor choice.

"I'm evolving!" Cleo shouted.

Norah held up her hand. "She *was* a pixie. I swear. Then she was cursed into crate form, and now she's a flying crate. If we can track down some brainwood, she'll be a flying crate with hands."

"Brainwood?" The eyes widened, the pupils dilating in surprise. The elf's voice darkened. "How did you find me?"

"We really *are* friends with Stellan. Or Cleo and Madge

are. I'm fighting my way back into his good graces." Norah watched the elf warily. "You know Stellan, right? Increasingly luxurious red beard? Bit of a temper?"

The bowstring relaxed another millimeter, and wary interest bloomed on the wood elf's brown skin. "I can't make any promises, but if you hand over your wands, we can have a chat like civilized people."

Madge's face was unenthusiastic. Norah checked her emotional radar. Yolen had no appetite for violence, though he did appear to be hungry. "I have some granola bars if you want to break bread," she offered.

He nodded sharply.

Norah and Madge laid their wands on the ground. Yolen stored them carefully with his quiver of arrows and motioned them toward the sunfruit tree. Just outside the reach of the yellow light, blackened stones surrounded the cold remains of a campfire. Yolen used a bow drill to set a small pile of moss smoldering, then added twigs and larger sticks. Soon a comfortable fire was blazing. Norah set her granola bars on a nearby rock.

"I snare rabbits now and again, but we are very close to the city. The health of the ecosystem here is balanced on a blade's edge." Pulling a vicious silver knife from a sheath at his belt, he cut off a slice of ripe sunfruit and handed it graciously to Madge before tossing the rest to Norah.

Low wooden benches piled with cushions surrounded the fire. Nearby, carved poles held a handmade tent canopy aloft. The poles were covered in a sticky black sap that looked disgusting but smelled like a distilled Christmas tree.

"How long have you lived here?" Norah asked.

"Since 1972," Yolen said. "Cornelius grew this forest, and I appointed myself its guardian."

"Is Cornelius the crazy botanist?"

The wood elf's eyes locked on her. "He wasn't crazy. He was a maestro of forestry."

From an ordinary person, that would have been high praise. From a wood elf, it was quasi-religious adulation.

"Other people thought he was crazy, though," Norah stated.

"That's true. When he came through my people's forest in Oriceran, I was a young ranger. I was sent to track him and expel him from our land. I caught up with him in less than half a day. He loved the outdoors, but he was not athletic.

"He asked me astute questions about various plant species and their properties as I escorted him from the forest. He'd point in a direction, and I'd go there and answer his questions. Then he'd point in another direction. We moved continuously toward the forest's border without ever reaching it.

"I followed him back to Earth and asked him to take me on as an apprentice. Over the course of a three-day trip, he collected an astonishing number of cuttings and seeds. He scraped the dirt off his shoes and planted it in case it had picked up anything interesting."

"Had it?" Norah asked.

"Oh, yes. That sunfruit tree, for instance. This whole acre is pure Oriceran, or it started that way. Before he experimented with hybrids."

"How come no one's ever caught you?" Madge asked. Sunfruit juice dribbled down her face.

Norah nodded. "Someone must have stumbled across this campsite. A ranger, or an enthusiastic bushwhacker, or college kids on psychedelics."

"This area is heavily warded with camouflage magic. You shouldn't have been able to see it."

Cleo glowed so brightly that specks of rune were visible through the net bag. "Like I said. I'm an original."

Yolen chuckled. "It's funny you mention psychedelics. Cornelius did sometimes bring friends here after they took LSD. He showed off his life's work, and they thought it was all part of the drug experience."

The site had been constructed with care, but Yolen clearly didn't get many visitors. He must be lonely. "When Cornelius died, why did you stay?" Norah asked.

"Because this is a special place, and Oriceran has had its share of wars. My people's forest has burned down several times. This acre is a magical-botanical library."

"Like the Svalbard seed vault."

Yolen nodded. "Cornelius snuck some magical seed packets into Svalbard, too. That part of Earth is too cold to interest me. Now that relations between humans and magicals are more open, I've thought about revealing this preserve, but I've gotten used to the solitude."

"So, do you really grow brainwood here?" Norah asked.

Yolen stood. Specks of sunfruit juice cast an eerie glow across his mouth.

"Come with me." With a swift motion, he snapped off a branch laden with bright fruit and held it before him like a torch. The bobbing light illuminated strange branches and leaves of all colors and textures. Norah steered around a carnivorous plant with a wide pink mouth that she decided should be called a Venus Pomeranian trap.

"Here we are." Yolen jammed the makeshift torch into the dirt.

At first, she thought the wood elf had taken them to an empty clearing. Yolen bent down next to a fist-sized plant in the tilled earth. She took a knee beside him.

It was obvious where the plants had gotten their name. The trunks were intricately folded, and the pale bark was shot through with black stripes that twisted in dizzying patterns. Like a brain, the trunks had two hemispheres. Dense clusters of pinhead-sized leaves grew from the central cleft like a mohawk. They were magical, glowing with an inner light that filled the trunks.

Norah whistled a few bars of *Puttin' on the Ritz*, and the leaves shivered.

"These are fifty years old?" she asked, struggling to keep the disappointment out of her voice.

"No." Yolen straightened, looking protective. "Those are three hundred years old. When I came to Earth, I transplanted several young trees."

"You mean you stole them." Madge snorted.

"Well, yes. These over here are the ones we grew from seeds." He pulled up the branch and held it over a patch of dirt twenty feet away. After following him, Norah had to squint to see the marble-sized orbs. "It's part of why I've never been back. My people guard their brainwood carefully."

As Norah stared at the globes, she realized they weren't glowing. She wasn't seeing the light with her eyes. She was seeing it with her radio magic.

When Norah used her empathic radar, people's intentions flowed to her in currents and waves, scraps of desire and intention licking out. These trees didn't *have* emotions; they *were* emotions. Whatever the substance was that carried thinking creatures' desires to Norah, this wood was filled to the brim with it. She now understood why it was so valuable.

"How big do the plants get?"

Yolen shrugged. "In my infancy, I saw one that was twice the height of my father. He was tall for a wood elf. They grow until someone cuts them down, and someone *always* cuts them down." He sounded sad, and Norah felt guilty about her mission. "That's why I planted them so far apart. I'd like to study their magical-botanical properties in a secure environment."

"I don't suppose you'd let any of the wood go?" Norah asked. "For, say, a pixie in need."

A coyote howled in the silence, and a dark shape swooped out of the forest in the distance and flew over the camp. Its speed increased, the dark shape a blur.

"Is that an owl?" Norah asked uneasily. She realized she wasn't the one who needed to be afraid. "Oh, shit."

Madge screamed as the predatory brown-winged bird swooped into the light and snatched her in mid-hover with its long talons.

"*Madge!*" Norah screamed.

Yolen was on his feet before Madge stopped screaming. She had left a defensive cloud of glittering pixie dust in the air, and before the owl was halfway through a dazed hoot, Yolen loosed an arrow into the darkness.

"Be careful!" Norah plunged into the forest after a howl

of pain. Yolen, faster and more familiar with the territory, sprinted past. When she caught up with him, he was bent over a screeching, flailing bird. Norah searched for Madge, but a confusion of feathers blocked her view.

"My wand!" she shouted. Yolen tossed her the canister. Norah yanked the lid off and shot a succession of stunning spells into the bird. Its wings stilled in mid-flap. A scrap of neon-yellow peeked out from between its talons.

Madge's body was motionless, and Norah nearly vomited as she crept forward before recognizing the pixie's familiar frozen expression. She'd been hit by one of Norah's stunning spells. Her left wing was shredded, and a gash along her side dripped dark-green pixie blood on the ground. The pool was almost the size of Madge's head.

Norah pulled every scrap of energy from her body and the surrounding environment and twined it into an egg of healing blue magic, which she closed gently around the pixie. The instant the gash on Madge's side stopped bleeding, Norah reversed the stunning spell.

"Fucking owls!" Madge screamed, as ornery as ever. More beautiful words had never been spoken.

Norah was desperate to hug her friend, but with pixies, there was a very fine line between hugging and crushing in one's fist, so she held off.

"Your Gucci tracksuit is ruined," Norah stated flatly. She'd used all the energy in her body, and her mind was blank.

"It was a knockoff," Madge whispered.

Yolen murmured, and Norah realized he was talking to the owl. The arrow had taken it through the wing, and

Yolen was applying pressure to the wound against his body as he struggled to retrieve a jar of salve from his waist.

"My wand," Madge said.

Norah fished the toothpick-sized wand out of Yolen's canister and handed it to her. She assumed the pixie wanted to work on her wings, but a thread of light shot from the tiny wand into the wound on the owl's shoulder. The owl's eyes were almost too dark to read, but a hint of surprise might have flickered across them.

"Don't think this means we're friends. The next time I see you, I'm going to punch the feathers off your face. You won't get the drop on me twice." Her voice sounded very tired, and the thread of magic petered out. "This is why I don't go hiking."

The owl had quieted, and Norah inspected the tear in Madge's papery wing. If her torso had taken that damage, she might not have survived. It would take a long time to heal.

"I'm going to buy you so many lion tamarin shifter massages." Norah wiped her hand across the back of her eyes.

"We should go back to the fire, where it's warm." Yolen cradled the owl in his arms as they walked through the forest.

The bird's eyes went wide when it saw the campfire, and Madge glowered. "It would serve you right, but owl meat tastes like shit," the pixie muttered.

Yolen placed the bird on the ground a safe distance from the flames.

"What did you do to it?" he asked Madge. "There's a very strange look in its eyes."

"It sniffed a fierce burst of pixie dust," Madge's voice was barely audible above the crackling campfire. "Buddy-o's having a wild ride through the maximum hallucinatory capabilities of his birdbrain."

Norah chuckled. Pepe crept toward Madge, the pink tip of his tongue emerging from his mouth.

"Pepe! No licking Madge without her permission. And even if she said yes, now is not the time for a drug trip."

Yolen laughed, a low sound like leaves rippling in the wind. Sighing, he removed the woven bag from his shoulder and released the drawstring. Cleo flapped out feet-first, then righted herself as she swooped down to check on Madge.

Yolen watched. "Cleo, you are the one who requires the brainwood?"

Cleo's two carved runes that resembled eyes gleamed. "If I'm going to be the next Roger Deakins, opposable thumbs would be mighty convenient."

Norah raised her eyebrows, and Cleo whacked her with a transparent wing. "Not right at first, you know. I will put my immortality to good use."

Yolen placed his chin in one hand and stared into the fire.

"One of my brainwood saplings refuses to flourish. A nearby strangleroot is disturbing its soil. I could give you that tree." Norah sat up, and the glow from the fire brightened Yolen's face. His eyes flickered with dark emotions. "Under two conditions."

Norah's guts clenched. First Arret had money in the bank since *The Players* had wrapped, but it wasn't a dragon's hoard.

Yolen unrolled the cuff of one brown pant leg and unbuttoned a small pouch at the hem. From it, he withdrew three seeds. They were the size of lima beans but a much brighter green, almost neon. "I want you to plant these for me."

Pepe trotted up and sniffed the seeds but made no attempt to eat them, which was as damning an indictment as any magical test she could have run.

Norah raised an eyebrow. "The garden at my apartment complex is small. I'll have to check with Stan."

Yolen shook his head. "I need you to plant them somewhere specific. When Cornelius came back from Oriceran, he described his experiences to a colleague in the botany department at Los Angeles University. The man believed him, especially when he saw Cornelius's samples, but smelled an opportunity for advancement.

"They were both up for tenure the following year. Dr. Gilroy had Cornelius committed to a mental institution, and when he was released, the department fired him. Gilroy is a fossil now, but he's still at the university. It galls me. I would like you to plant these seeds in his office."

"His office?" Norah asked. From the way Yolen said Gilroy's name, she doubted the seeds grew into harmless flowers.

The owl emitted a soft noise. "Hoot hoot!" The stunning spell was starting to wear off.

Yolen nodded. "You four have proven to be very resourceful. I am sure you can find a way."

"What's the second condition?" Cleo asked.

"When the hands are complete, I'd like you to visit me. I haven't seen brainwood in action since my childhood. I would take a few notes and observe your dexterity. Truthfully, I might also put you to work. This little forest garden is difficult to care for by myself."

Cleo's runes glowed meditatively, then she flapped into the air and bobbed in a sort of bow.

"You've got yourself a deal, mister. Er, if someone's willing to plant the seeds."

"You don't need special equipment," Yolen said cheerfully. "Merely stick the seeds in the soil and water them with elf tears. The plant will do the rest."

Norah grinned when she remembered that Frondle could cry on cue. *Thank you, method acting.*

"I can handle it. I'm sure Frondle will help."

"I bet he'd love to plant a few seeds," Madge said before her ribaldry turned into a vicious coughing fit. Norah needed to get Madge home.

"Hoot!" The cry was louder.

"You should leave before the old man gets back to normal. He'll probably be angry as he adjusts to the injury," Yolen locked eyes with the owl.

"Any chance you can give us directions? We're slightly lost," Norah pleaded.

"Don't listen to her," Cleo muttered. "We're *totally* lost."

Yolen fished in a small satchel at his belt and retrieved a black leaf covered in blacker sap. "Chew this. It's pathfinder sage. It will link you to the interconnected root network of the forest. You'll know where to go. Once you've completed the planting, return to me for the brainwood."

"Do you need proof? I can take photos," Norah offered.

Yolen's mouth quirked cryptically. "Believe me, I'll know."

It wasn't reassuring. Norah scraped the black sap on the sage leaf with a fingernail, and a pungent musk wafted up.

"Down the hatch," Cleo said cheerfully.

"Hoot hoot!" The owl was decidedly more threatening this time, and Norah high-tailed into the forest as Yolen waved. Pepe trotted behind, with Madge lying across his back. The trees enfolded Norah in darkness, which on the plus side, made the strange-smelling leaf impossible to see as she stuffed it into her mouth and swallowed.

The forest was cool and dark except for a single spot in the distance. A small tree appeared to be beckoning her closer, so she moved toward it. "We're trying to get back to the parking lot," Norah stated. The tree shivered, and in the distance, another swayed, crooking a branch.

"Great. She's talking to trees now." Madge's voice barely carried above Pepe's hoofbeats.

"I didn't see anyone else offering to eat the weird leaf," Norah stated. The velvety leaves of a lamb's ear plant waved her on. With the aid of their botanical guides, they moved quickly, and the lights of the ranger station soon appeared in the distance. Norah touched the pocket of her yoga pants, in which three small seeds resided.

Bartering for magic beans. What could possibly go wrong?

CHAPTER NINETEEN

The botany building at Los Angeles University had been dark and quiet for at least half an hour. Norah was restless. She had many interesting ideas about how to spend two hours in a dark car with Frondle, none of which included staring through binoculars at a pair of double doors. Aggrieved, she downed the last dregs of her gas station coffee. "Let's go. I think the place is empty, or empty enough."

Frondle followed her as they crept across the quad.

The keycard lock on the door was easy to open with a simple rune. Even if the university believed in magic, they hadn't wised up to its dangers. Motion sensors turned on ugly fluorescent lights above them as they traversed the hallways, looking for Professor Gilroy's office. They found it on the second floor. This door was made of heavy oak, but it, too, was easy to breach.

Inside, they faced another problem. The office was stuffed with books about plants, diagrams of plants, and elegant nineteenth-century botanical illustrations. There was a blown glass orchid under a dome in the corner of the room. There were no living plants, however.

Norah scoffed. "This guy calls himself a botanist." She checked the trashcan, hoping Gilroy was the kind of person who killed a bromeliad every few months, but no luck. "I noticed some plants by the bathrooms. Wait here?"

Frondle nodded. He was flipping through a book on herbal medicine.

Norah crept down the hallway toward a leafy green potted plant. Upon reaching it, however, she discovered it was fake. The reproduction was so exact that it took her a moment to realize.

"Disgraceful," she muttered.

"Hey! What are you doing?"

Norah straightened as a janitor aggressively pushed a mop bucket toward her. The woman appeared to be in her early forties and had a faint Eastern European accent. She seemed to be exhausted.

Norah took a step back. "I'm, um, inspecting this tree for pests."

"That's not a real tree," the janitor stated.

Damn. Norah smiled brightly. "Exactly. There's an invasive Oriceran bug called the, um, bottle beetle. It eats plastic."

"That's not plastic. It's silk." The janitor's hand moved to her walkie-talkie. "Those are expensive to replace, you know. I'm sure your dorm room looks barren, but that's no excuse for larceny."

"I'm not a student." Norah was offended on behalf of her luxurious Oriceran hybrids.

"Oh, really?" The walkie-talkie was now gripped in a fist.

Shit. Stupid ego. Think, Wintry. "I'm a, uh, adjunct. In the bug science department."

"Bug science." The woman became more skeptical.

What was the word? An analog clock ticked on a nearby wall.

"Entomology!" Norah shouted, then clapped her hand over her mouth.

"Adjunct, huh? Sorry to hear it. They pay you people less than me. My advice? Unionize.

"All right, well, I can't encourage theft, but I stand in solidarity with the academic underclass. Let's say that if you want to steal that tree. The camera at the side entrance is out and I won't be working in this hallway again for another twenty minutes." She smiled and tapped her nose.

"Thanks." Norah pulled her hoodie over her face at the mention of security cameras. "I'm not trying to steal this tree, by the way."

"Sure, you're not!" The janitor winked and strolled away.

"How is it this hard to find soil in the botany department?" Norah murmured under her breath.

As she spoke, she noticed the base of the silk tree. It might have been fake, but real dirt covered the base. *Bingo.*

She cast an antigrav spell on the pot and pushed it ahead of her into the office.

Frondle smiled when she popped out from behind the branches. When he rubbed one of the leaves between his fingers, however, he frowned.

"Norah?" he asked hesitantly, staring at the silk.

"I know it's not real." Norah drew a small circle in the air with her wand and sent the glowing blue lines spinning. The magical blade cut through the plastic, which emitted a tendril of acrid smoke.

"We don't need a real plant. Only real dirt." As Frondle watched, she ran her fingers through the shallow soil.

"Why would someone plant a fake plant in real dirt?"

"To make it look more real."

"If they wanted a real plant, couldn't they buy a real plant?"

Norah pointed at the pot. "It's your time to shine. All we need to complete the planting is an elf's tears, and I'm lucky enough to have an extremely talented client who can weep on cue."

Frondle stared at his elven boots, which were covered in small scales and glistened like an oil spill. "Maybe we could use water?"

"Yolen was very specific."

Frondle went to stand in the window, his face bathed in moonlight. "Do you know any other elves?" he asked.

"Not anyone who's available in the middle of the night on a Tuesday!" Norah cried. "What's going on? Are you dehydrated?"

"Madame Ploot says never to say no at an audition. Can you waterski? Yes. Will you wear this toxic silver paint? Yes. Can you cry on command? Yes."

"What did you do during filming?"

"Hair and makeup bought double-strength Oriceran hybrid Vedalia onions. I kept one in my pocket. It was very draining."

Norah rubbed her eyes. "This plan was contingent on you being able to cry on cue! It's why I brought you!"

Frondle's chin wobbled, and Norah felt a guilty surge of delight. A cruel idea rose unbidden in her mind. *Remember. This is for Cleo's hands.*

She crossed her arms across her chest. "You think Daniel Day-Lewis struggles to cry on command? You think Meryl Streep has trouble? No! When Spielberg says 'Cry,' Tom Hanks is a fucking waterfall! Did you think you'd be able to make it in Hollywood with those Atacama deserts you call eyes?"

The chin quiver became a full-on earthquake. Beads of moisture distorted Frondle's icy blue irises. *Whoa, Wintry. One more.*

"I'm releasing you as a client." She dropped it like a bomb, voice low and chin raised. Frondle's face made her regret the ruse. He deflated.

A teardrop hovered precipitously on a blond lash. He raised a hand to wipe it away.

"No!" Norah shouted. "Into the pot!"

Frondle, understanding dawning, leaned over the pot as the droplet fell. As it sank into the newly-disturbed soil, the grains shivered. After several more drops had hit the soil, Norah pulled Frondle to his feet.

"I'm so sorry. I'm not releasing you as a client." She flung her arms around the elf, but he remained stiff.

"Is that true about Daniel Day-Lewis?" Frondle sniffed.

"Of course not!" She leaned in conspiratorially. "Chanel makes a special pepper perfume that he sprays in his eyes between takes."

The first hint of a smile appeared on Frondle's lips. "Really?"

Norah smiled. "Absolutely," she lied.

"So, you didn't bring me to cry on the seeds?"

The plastic pot jolted an inch across the floor, startling Norah. She stepped back, alarmed, as a green shoot burst from the pot.

Norah put her hands on Frondle's shoulders. "I wanted to see you, but it's hard to spend time together without, you know, wanting to tear your elven armor off."

Frondle's cautious happiness turned offended. "As if you'd be able to! The craftsmanship is incomparable."

Norah grinned. "Well, I'd have fun trying." Frondle's eyes glinted, but not with tears. "And I want to respect your oath. I know it's important to you."

Frondle swept her into his arms. "Dark Hound *will* fall. My oath is not as important as—"

There was a crash, and specks of plaster rained on Norah's head.

"Holy shit." The sprouting plant, which had been two inches tall when she'd started talking to Frondle, had hit the ceiling.

A smooth, verdant stalk as wide around as a hubcap supported twining offshoots that ended in heart-shaped leaves. The flurry of brilliant growth made Norah's eyes hurt.

Wood creaked as the pressure of the stalk against the plaster increased, and hardwood bowed below them. Whatever they had planted was about to punch the roof off this building.

Frondle pulled a beam of yellow light from the overhead fluorescents and shattered the nearest window in a kaleidoscope of flying glass. The beam of light flopped over the sill and down the side of the building, a makeshift rope. As Frondle ushered her toward it, a voice rang out from the hallway.

"What on earth?" The words were barely audible above the whine of strain as the plant's stalk thickened and roots burst out of the pot.

"The janitor!" Norah ran into the hallway. Frondle moved to follow, but an explosion of offshoots blocked his path. "Go! I'll meet you outside!" she screamed. When a small piece of rebar hit the floor beside her, she cast a protective shield over her head.

Foot-wide fissures shot across the marble floor as she spilled out into the hallway, splitting the marble into shaky islands. The janitor balanced on one of these, mop limp at her side. The bucket had plummeted through the crack.

"Jump!" Norah gestured at a clear spot fifteen feet distant. The janitor looked at her like she was crazy.

Shit. Norah released the shield and shot an antigrav spell into her tennis shoes as she leapt the gap to the janitor's chunk of floor. Looking at the mop, she had an idea.

"Get on the mop!" she shouted. "Don't worry. I'm a witch."

Dazed, the janitor hooked a leg over. Norah jumped on behind her, recasting the antigrav spell as the floor dropped out from under them.

"Ow! Fuck!"

Whatever witch had invented the concept of riding on broomsticks had hopefully invented the concept of padded underwear shortly after. Still, it was better than being crushed by a magic beanstalk-compromised botany building. They flew out the side hallway and rounded the corner, where Frondle stared up at the green monstrosity poking out of the building. It was now three stories tall, and its growth showed no signs of stopping.

"You're riding a broomstick!" Frondle cried as they dropped in a heap onto the grass. "I thought that was a cliche for people who didn't have access to couture."

A twining offshoot punched out the window she had looked out minutes before. Splinters of glass reflected the starlight from Frondle's hair.

"I might have been overly judgmental," Norah admitted.

"It's not a broomstick. It's a mop." The janitor clambered to her feet. "You weren't here to steal a fake tree, were you?"

"Er, no. Sorry."

"Are you kidding?" The janitor examined the building with bright eyes. "I'm trying to buy a condo, and you just gave me about a thousand hours of overtime. Besides, Professor Gilroy is a prick. He always calls me 'Mop Girl.' I'm forty-two!"

She gazed appreciatively at the explosion of tendrils and leaves. If anything, the growth was accelerating. The janitor turned back. "I'd get out of here before Campus Security shows up. And, you know, the police. I'm going to tell them Gilroy planted some weird seeds last night. Should be fun!"

Norah and Frondle made a beeline for her car, waving as they left.

When she pulled up in front of his apartment, his blue eyes searched hers.

"I don't think you should come up. Even after I have

fulfilled my oath, it's not good for you to be my agent and my lover, and I don't want to lose you as my agent."

The air in the car was suddenly very dense, and Norah resisted an urge to shout, "Are you breaking up with me?"

"When Dark Hound is gone, I think we should date in secret," Frondle continued. Norah let out a huge breath.

"A forbidden romance?" she asked.

He nodded gravely. "I have a gift for you. Wait here." He disappeared into his apartment building. A moment later, he emerged holding a tube carved from alternating stripes of white bone and black volcanic glass.

"This is a famous epic poem about a dark elf princess and a light elf knight who fall in love and are forced to conceal their feelings. It is widely regarded as one of the greatest works of elvish romantic poetry."

He checked the car, then leaned close. "It's also very sexy," he whispered. Norah grinned. "I keep wanting more art for my office. Though, it's not illustrated, is it?"

Frondle shook his head. "This one isn't. Would you like an illustrated edition? They can be very detailed."

"No, no. I'd rather not follow Harry Bing's example and cover the walls of my office in erotic art."

"I've heard unsettling stories," Frondle agreed. "Send my regards to Madge. How is her wing healing?"

Norah stared out the window. "The webbing hasn't regrown yet. I don't know if it will. She's been in a worse mood than the cantankerose, and she's riding Pepe like a warhorse. What worries me is that he's letting her."

Concerned that hugging the tall light elf would lead to additional oathbreaking, she patted his hand and placed the scroll carefully between them. Following his gaze out the window, she took a sharp breath.

A green glow in the sky framed the faint outline of a colossal twining tower visible from seven miles away. *The beanstalk.*

"When Yolen said he'd know if I planted the seeds, I thought he meant, like, some kind of secret plant signal," Norah stated. The stalk was pretty, but even from this distance, it was visible, growing into the overhead haze.

CHAPTER TWENTY

The truck stalled for the tenth time, and Norah cursed under her breath. She'd had to do a lot of stupid things in Hollywood. When she'd been an assistant, her boss had once asked her to dye his rottweiler like a tiger for Halloween.

She'd never tried anything as terrible as learning to drive a stick shift.

"Take a deep breath, push in the clutch, and put it in first gear," Lincoln said. "You'll get it this time."

"Isn't there a spell that can turn this thing into an automatic?" Norah asked as the car lurched forward and died.

"Ease off the clutch next time," Lincoln counseled.

Morin, who was cuffed into heavy wooden gloves that prevented her from manipulating anything bigger than a ball bearing, groaned from the backseat.

"You reaaally need a commercial driver's license to drive my trucks," she moaned.

"I do!" Norah said, pointing to the glamoured piece of plastic on the dashboard.

"I mean a real one," Morin shot back.

"It really *looks* like a Class A CDL!"

"I'm sure that'll be helpful when you drive a truck full of eggplants to the Humpr building."

"That will have a certain poetic irony." Norah glanced at the rearview mirror.

Morin rolled her eyes. "How have you lived in LA so long without knowing how to drive?"

"I also don't know how to send a fax or light a fire under a witch's cast iron cauldron," Norah added.

"Is that a real thing?" Morin asked.

"Faxes? Personally, I think my mom made them up to prank me."

Lincoln, riding patiently in the driver's seat, sighed. Before discovering that Norah couldn't drive a stick, Morin had called the Humpr offices and told them she had the flu. Their new farmhand would be making the delivery.

"How do I look?" Norah asked.

Morin smeared a streak of dirt across Norah's shirt and nodded.

"Are you sure he won't recognize me? If he's done research into my parents, he might know who I am."

"You're not wearing makeup," Morin stated grimly. "I guarantee he won't look at you."

Norah tried not to take it personally.

She also tried not to get distracted by the wide variety of magical produce Petra was loading into the truck. She plucked a pale white orb shot through with red from the pile and almost popped it into her mouth, then a large green stalk appeared in her peripheral vision. Sighing, Norah dropped the fruit and glanced back.

"One of my farming friends from the Bay is on the beanstalk task force," Lincoln told them. "It's still getting taller, but the diameter isn't increasing. It's past the troposphere already. I've heard NASA's Jet Propulsion Lab is considering using beanstalks as space elevators."

Norah brightened at the prospect of the towering plant having a purpose other than revenge.

She finally managed to drive the produce truck around the parking lot two or three times. "Time to hit the road."

"I hope you die on the highway!" Morin cried cheerfully, scratching her chin awkwardly with one wooden glove.

Humpr's headquarters took up a huge, wedge-shaped building in Santa Monica, an expanse of white walls and glass arches. It was one of four buildings surrounding a puddle of lifeless ponds crisscrossed by austere concrete walkways. Norah drove to the loading dock in the back, where a security guard checked her plates against a list on a tablet and waved her into a spot. A chipper woman with a purple mohawk wheeled out a cart stacked with coolers and shook Norah's hand.

"Hey! I'm Sedona. I'm the office manager. The coolers are for Mr. Forester's personal produce. Everything else goes on the cart."

She flipped open the top of one of the coolers and waited expectantly. They stared at each other until Sedona stated, "Morin usually does all the loading. It's part of the deal."

Norah wasn't too proud to do manual labor, and stalling wouldn't get her to the heart of Dark Hound. Desperate, she grabbed the nearest produce basket.

"Morin told me to take this directly to Cook."

"Tomatoes?" Sedona poked the basket with a neon-green nail. Something seemed off about the paint, but Norah didn't have time to focus.

"Tomatoes? Definitely not. These are Oriceran heart berries."

Sedona raised an eyebrow. Norah tried to remember some of the tech lingo that had been aggressively spoken at her on her mediocre Humpr dates.

"It's a...nootropic meal-replacement vegifruit."

Sedona crossed her arms. "Really?"

"And they're caffeinated!"

Apparently, this was the magic word. Sedona leaned forward and reached into the basket.

Norah pulled away. "I don't know if you want to risk it. These things are crazy. The last time I ate one, I was up for four days, and I started a blog about organic farming."

Was she getting through? Norah flicked on her radio magic to check. Emotion flowed into her from Sedona. The woman was afraid. Not of her, though. She was worried about Cook Forester.

Sedona shrugged and snagged one of the fruits. "Oh, man. This tastes like a tomato."

That's because it is.

"Crazy, huh?" Norah asked. "That's part of the appeal. You can stick it in a salad or turn it into nootropic caffeinated gazpacho."

"But it's not actually a tomato? Cook doesn't do nightshades."

"No, no. It looks and tastes exactly like a tomato. For synergy."

Sedona nodded wisely. "Synergy. So important."

"I'm supposed to give the produce only to him. If he's not free, I can come another time. I don't know how much longer they'll be in season."

A bright spike of anxiety hit Norah. "No, don't do that. If you're willing to sign an NDA, I can take you through."

Sedona took her into a lobby and pulled up a thirty-page document on a tablet. Norah held the down arrow and found the signature line.

"You're not going to read it?" Sedona sounded judgmental.

"I've got a lot to do today." Sedona shrugged as Norah, blanking on the name she'd put on her license, scribbled a series of illegible loops.

"Come with me," Sedona cut through the office toward the elevators. They passed so many ping-pong tables on the way up to the C-suite that Norah wondered if Humpr had a side hustle as a sporting goods factory.

Someone in a gray hoodie pulled down to his nose stopped Sedona to complain that the cafeteria was out of overnight oats. As she passed offices, she picked up hints of anxiety. What was going on with these people? Cautiously, she extended the reach of her emotional radar.

She preferred to keep the radio magic on low. Getting bonked in the head with every petty grievance within a half-mile radius was exhausting, but knowing what was going on in this building might save her parents' lives. She took a deep breath and pushed the range to its limits.

The emotional temperature in the building wasn't much different from what she'd felt at, say, an audition. Low-grade stress pervaded, and a colorless exhaustion fogged the atmosphere. A thread of ferocious anger also reached her. From the ground floor? No, she would have noticed it if she had passed it. It was deeper than that, separated from the other currents of emotion as if by a barrier. Maybe solid rock.

As they approached Cook's office, Sedona's anxiety ramped up, and she breathed harder.

"Can I use the restroom?" Norah blurted. "Sorry. It was a long drive from Ojai, and I ate too many heart berries."

A mixture of relief and annoyance flowed from Sedona. "It's down the hall." Norah smiled gratefully. After she rounded the corner, she sprinted back to the elevator and pressed the button for the lowest floor, Sub-basement Three.

The several employees who got on, scruffily-dressed men in their twenties, ignored her, except for one who noticed her basket of tomatoes. "The fourth-floor snacka-torium is out of kiwi," he mumbled without looking her in the eye.

"I'll get right on that," Norah stated.

The elevator creaked to its final stop and let her out into a cold hall full of locked doors. Norah spelled a few open but found only cleaning supplies and stored office furniture. Very little noise reached her ears, and less emotion reached her radar. Had she gone too far? She probed the surrounding ether, stretching her senses in all directions.

A ball of intense anger erupted near her feet. This time, it wasn't alone. Somewhere beneath her, a flurry of activity moved through a large, rectangular space. There must be another floor. Norah moved quickly down the hall, tapping locks with her wand, but none of them led to a staircase or a separate elevator.

She was so focused on the antlike emotional blips beneath that the ball of anger and threat of violence moving toward her from the elevator almost slipped past her radar.

Norah spun and shot a stunning spell blindly as Sedona raised a small blue plastic pistol. Sedona dove away from the stun and rolled expertly across the floor. Norah flung a shield up an instant before the two prongs of a taser gun slammed against it. The magic crackled under the surge of power and faded, and Sedona kicked Norah's arm up as she raised her wand. She almost lost her grip but had enough wherewithal to knee the woman between the legs.

Sedona grunted. "Get lost?" She did a complicated movement with her legs that sent Norah tumbling to the floor.

"This is outside the scope of an office manager," Norah stated in a strained voice as Sedona got her in a headlock. She struggled to move her wand into position, but Sedona tightened her grip. There was something strange about her arms, an inhuman hardness and weight.

Norah's airway was now cut off. Time was running out. In desperation, she tossed her wand in a half-circle like a juggler, reversing the tip and shooting a stunning spell wildly behind her. It connected, and relief flooded her as Sedona's arms stiffened. The relief lasted half a second before she realized Sedona's arms were locked in place over her windpipe.

Her mouth formed "Fuck," but no sound emerged.

If she unfroze Sedona, she would die. The woman

would crush her windpipe before she could get her wand up. The violence wasn't personal. The cold intention flowing into Norah's emotional senses was reminiscent of the lizard-brain killing instinct of Morin's alligator. Black crawled from the edges of Norah's vision, and with an intense stab of guilt, she pointed her wand skyward, raised a spinning blue blade of magic, and sent it through Sedona's left arm. The world exploded back into focus as the pressure on her neck released, and Norah, tumbling away from her, cast a coagulation spell into the stump of Sedona's arm. There was little blood on the floor, which was a relief.

Actually, there was *no* blood. That was an impossibility, no matter how cleanly her magic had cut. Norah reached for the stump and found it cold to the touch. The severed end, far from bloody, was a bright circle of gold, and the limb was too heavy to lift. Paint flaked off under her grip, and metal shone lustrously from beneath.

Norah gaped. "Is that...solid gold?"

Sedona was still frozen, but the surge of anger flowing into her suggested her guess was right. It seemed impossible. The arm had moved like living flesh, and Sedona was strong, but no one was *that* strong.

Was the woman an advanced robot? Confused, she laid a palm against Sedona's forehead. Her skin was warm. Norah unfroze her mouth.

"What are you?" she asked.

Cool anger spat back. "I'm not telling you anything. Security will be here in seconds to end your pathetic attempt at corporate espionage."

Corporate espionage? Apparently, Sedona didn't know

who she was. Norah shot an antigrav spell into the arm. Flakes of tan paint fell off as it rose into the air. She shoved the gleaming, disembodied limb toward the elevator.

"I might not have learned any thrilling corporate secrets, but I'm sure my employers will be equally happy with a metric fuck-ton of gold. Or maybe I'll go as a super-authentic King Tut for Halloween." Raising the heavy object took a huge amount of energy. If Sedona called her bluff, she'd be running on fumes before she reached the elevator.

"That's my life savings," Sedona snarled. "I don't trust banks."

Norah, gritting her teeth under what she hoped was a nonchalant smirk, floated the arm casually back to the floor, breathing easier once it was down.

"I'm a metal elemental. I lost my arm in a skiing accident when I was a kid, and gold is the only metal soft enough to manipulate. I tried latex sacks of mercury, but they kept breaking. My cat almost died. The arm was part of my compensation package. They matched my contribution."

"Aren't you worried about someone stealing it?" Norah asked.

Sedona shook her head. "I'm not defenseless."

The hall full of dead-end doors stretched coldly beyond them. The flurry of deeper activity hadn't slowed.

"How do I get to the basement?" Norah asked. "The *real* basement."

Surprise registered on Sedona's face. As she opened her mouth, Norah felt three balls of professional violent intention descending in the elevator. Somewhere in the building, an alarm sounded.

"Here's what we're going to do," Norah said. "You're going to send them down the hall, and I'm going to leave your arm here. I haven't checked the price of gold lately, but I'm sure it's a motivating sum. If you don't play along, I'm going to let them capture me and tell them you were my inside source for building access."

Fear for both her professional reputation and her life burst out of the woman. Cook Forester would have her killed. Even if he didn't, breaking her NDA came with devastating financial consequences. Blood draining out of her face, she gave a shallow nod.

Norah cast an antigrav spell on Sedona's body and propped her in a standing position. It seemed slapdash, so she added a glamour to make her good arm point down the hall.

It would have to do. Norah slipped into a closet near the elevator, pushing the door shut as the elevator disgorged its contents. People emerged, and a deep male voice shot a question down the hall.

Come on, Sedona. Come through.

"She's in there," Sedona shouted. Heavy boots thundered toward her and Norah slipped out, padded into the elevator, and slid out of view behind the door. She pressed the button for the lobby, inhaling when the doors closed and it rumbled up.

The truck was a lost cause. Morin would have to eat the loss. Abandoning it in the loading bay, Norah left the building at a sprint and veered down a bike path toward the ocean. When she was a few miles away, she dashed into a café.

Ordering a coffee, Norah watched the barest segment of the shining blue line of the ocean between two buildings. She desperately wanted to call Madge, but the pixie didn't need more on her plate. She had harbored a secret hope that she'd be able to take out Dark Hound in her first attempt and return to her family a conquering hero, but she needed help.

CHAPTER TWENTY-ONE

Uriel had somehow added a second story to his rooftop encampment, a loft assembled from discarded furniture. It was covered in soft pillows, and a copy of *Neuromancer* lay open on a blanket.

"You like my reading nook?" he asked. The new structure was visible from the street.

Norah hoped she wouldn't have to answer any hard questions from building code enforcement, but that was a fight for another day.

"What have you found out about Humpr?" she asked.

"The company's aboveboard. Kinda gross but aboveboard. That 'office manager' was a ranked women's MMA fighter before she went into tech a few years ago. She's titled as a mid-level administrator, but she's paid as top-level security. Anti-espionage, probably."

"So, you didn't find anything?"

Uriel narrowed his eyes, and she shut her mouth. "Their security budget is two standard deviations higher than the average tech startup's, but it's not out of the question.

Those guys get paranoid. Forester's widely despised, and he knows it.

"There's something fishy going on with the building. I hacked into the Department of Water and Power's billing system. That place uses more electricity than the surrounding two-block radius combined."

"What does that mean?" Norah asked.

"It means it's not an office building. If I had to guess, it's a server farm. As I'm sure you noticed from my palace, underground locations have certain advantages."

"Cooling?"

Uriel nodded. "Though I doubt they have dope magical waterfall systems."

"He'll be on his guard now," she stated.

"Most definitely." Uriel typed rapidly, then met her gaze. "He spent lots of money on a security contractor that specializes in magical protection. It's a black-hat outfit that might reasonably be called a mercenary detachment."

"Shit."

"If you go after him, try not to miss." It was both a warning and practical advice.

Looking at the half-open book in Uriel's reading nook, Norah crossed her arms. "Stand up."

Uriel pulled his keyboard closer and inched away from her.

"I'm taking you to a party."

"I hate parties," Uriel said.

"Kim's is catering," Norah said. "I ordered four large banchan pizzas. Twice the number I brought you last time, per your demands."

Uriel looked up, interest stirring in his eyes.

"You can wear your mask," she added. "Come on! It'll freak out my guests. I know you love being a rooftop Henry David Thoreau, but I want you to meet my friends."

"Henry Thoreau's mother brought him sandwiches every day," Uriel muttered and glanced at the tardigrade mask hanging from a sawed-off coat rack under the awning. He reluctantly reached for the gaping mouth.

Madge and Pepe met Norah at the door to her apartment. The pixie was seated on a padded platform that had been secured to Pepe's back by a series of leather straps. Norah hoped she hadn't given up.

"Who made that for you?" she asked. Madge gazed past Norah's knees, and Pepe suddenly grew very interested in nibbling at the entrance's shoe rack. It must have been Stellan. He had done beautiful custom work for Cleo.

"Oh," Norah said. "I'm glad you two are still seeing each other. How are you feeling?"

"I have blisters!" Madge raised a dirty bare foot. "I have to walk everywhere like a chump, and every pair of shoes in my size is made for decoration over function. I had to go back to that hiking-obsessed fairy and shell out half my fucking salary for custom boots, which won't be ready for another two weeks."

Norah glanced cautiously at Madge's back. Glittering new growth had appeared along the edge of her shredded wing. Madge, following her eyes, grumbled. "Yolen sent me some salve. It smells like regurgitated sweat glands, but it's working."

"Norah!" a man called from the kitchen. Stan was holding a mixing bowl and wearing a dwarven forge apron made of thick leather plates stitched together with cooling runes. He was overdressed for suburban baking.

Ignoring the drops of batter on the enchanted leather, Norah threw her arms around him. "I missed you! How was Antarctica?"

"I almost lost a point to frostbite." Stan pointed at a delicate silk bandage around the tip of his left ear. "When I told Minnie I wanted to take long walks on the beach with her, I envisioned fewer emperor penguins. She loved it, though."

He shivered at the memory of the weather, and Norah patted his arm consolingly. "The heavy metal music festival was reasonably entertaining. Have you ever heard *I Worship the God of Death at a Temple Made of Frozen Bones*? It's very catchy."

"I'll check it out," Norah stated.

Stan gazed past her shoulder at the black-and-white tube leaning against her sofa.

"The *Tale of Scoria and Solarion*!" He leaned conspiratorially close and raised an interested eyebrow. "Is it illustrated?"

"No. I've been meaning to have it framed. And find a good translation."

Stan nodded. "My favorite part is when they fling themselves onto the jagged rocks of the Valley of Sorrow."

Norah's eyebrows inched up. "Frondle said it was a love story."

"Oh, it's very romantic," Stan agreed. "Their passion was

so fierce that it was worth starting a bloody intergenerational war between their families."

"I didn't realize they died."

"Well, they lived for several days, impaled upon the rocks. A lot of people think it's a metaphor for sex, but the poem is literal in that department. I think it's a meditation on the dangers of forbidden love." He scrutinized her.

Norah avoided his eyes and gazed at the lemon tree in the courtyard. "A warning about the draconewts would have been nice."

"Ah, yes. I noticed new burn marks on the tile."

Petra emerged from the kitchen with enough guacamole to swim in but almost dropped it when she followed Norah's gaze out the window. Uriel was standing in the shadows under the lemon tree, ominous in his mask and trench coat.

"Come meet Uriel," Norah said. "I think you'll like him." She checked her phone. It would be a half-hour until the brainwood arrived. Cleo flew around outside, offering a tray of Quint's mini quiches to the growing party in the garden. Next to the buffet table, Castor was attached at the hip to Sid and kept patting the leather satchel of tools at his side. Norah had assured him that no one expected him to assemble Cleo's new hands on the spot, but he had only half-believed her.

Norah took the guacamole from her mother, who warned her not to eat it all on the way out the door.

"I'm twenty-eight!" Norah shouted.

As she carried her precious cargo to the buffet, an azalea bush caught her eye. An odd, incongruous shimmer graced its edges. Norah put down the guacamole, squinted at the spot, and grabbed her wand. As she pointed it, squares of the azalea bush flipped over into brown skin, revealing a small wood elf. It was Yolen.

"How long have you been creeping in my azaleas?" Norah asked.

"I was early. Cornelius told me that being early to a party in Los Angeles is social suicide."

"He was right, but we'll make an exception." She was honored. She guessed the wood elf hadn't left his plot in a long time.

Yolen stared into the distance, and Norah followed his gaze to the large green stalk towering above Los Angeles

"It's coming along very well!" Yolen announced. "I wish I could get such prodigious growth out of my plants. Perhaps I could create some sort of hybrid."

Norah winced. As much as she hated to quell anyone's creativity, she could foresee poor outcomes from hybridizing the country's most ravenous and fast-growing plants. Colossal unstoppable poison oak sprouted in her imagination.

Rumors were spreading online that the beanstalk had hollowed out an enormous cave network beneath Los Angeles University, and mole people were living there. Learning about Oriceran had sent conspiracy theorists off the deep end. Yolen, basking in the distant green glow, smiled brightly.

"Quint is experimenting with a new way of cooking burgers that requires digging a pit in the yard, so no promises about dinner, but there's guacamole and mini quiches."

"I've got no-bake peanut butter balls," someone gruffly

stated from behind the wood elf. Stellan stood with his arms crossed, his flattened red beard reflecting a blinding amount of light.

"You came!" When Norah ran to hug him, she found herself barred by the smooth shaft of an axe.

"Stan and Cleo invited me. Unlike *others* in attendance, Stan and Cleo are my friends." Stellan glared across the lawn at Castor, who took a protective step behind a bowl of potato chips. "I see you invited the traitor."

"He's making Cleo's hands for her," Norah said. "Of course I invited him."

Air whooshed as Cleo rushed toward Stellan, wings flapping cheerfully. Norah barely managed to catch the tray of quiches that slid off her flat top as she high-fived the dwarf with one winged foot.

"Stellan! Castor showed me the new mockups for the hands. I signed up for piano lessons, and they should *just* be big enough. I hope they're ready in time for fall classes at UCLA. He has been working with Lottie like a madman to prep."

"Hello, Cleo," Yolen stated. The box, startled by his sudden appearance, lost elevation before recovering.

"Yolen! You came in person! Unless that's bad? Is there a problem?" Cleo's wings picked up speed as she hovered near him.

Yolen smiled. "No, no problem." He unstrung a small net bag from his hip. Inside, the tiny brainwood tree glowed with psychic energy.

Stellan whistled. Castor looked nervous as he reached for it, but his hand was steady as he gripped the small trunk.

Stellan's hand tightened on his axe. Norah hoped she wouldn't have to reattach a limb.

Castor cleared his throat.

"Stellan, I'm very sorry about what I did on the set of *The Players*. I hope you understand that I was only able to do as much damage as I did because your construction was so good."

"I know that," Stellan growled. His voice sounded like a lawnmower.

"Play nice," Cleo demanded. "I need my team to be a well-oiled dwarven construct."

Stellan nodded fractionally, and Castor swallowed.

"You sure you're up for this, kid?" Stellan asked.

Castor nodded decisively. "I'm one of Variety's Ten Young Puppeteers to Watch." He didn't sound certain, but Norah hoped for the best.

Quint and Andrew ambled in, and Jackie chased Leaf across the courtyard. Her nephew was wielding his elven blade. He waved it dramatically with a flash of bright metal as he ran to Norah, and she took a cautious half-step back.

"Mom said I could play swords with Frondle. Where is he?" Leaf asked.

There was a bright flash and a rustle of silk overhead, and Frondle descended from the sky on a sunbeam. Embroidered marigold silk of a traditional light elf style billowed as he lofted like a young god onto the grass. Leaf's face lit up almost as brightly as Frondle's robes, and he sprinted toward the light elf with his sword out, cheerfully screaming, "Taste Stephen!"

Norah was almost, but not quite, worried. Before Leaf came within chopping distance, Frondle produced a small dagger from a hidden sheath and deflected Leaf's attacks with precise parries, moving slowly enough that Leaf could see what he was doing and copy him. He looked away long enough to wink at Norah, and her heart rose an inch in her chest.

The party turned lively. Everyone but Castor ate and drank while Leaf, Stan, and Frondle engaged in casual sword fighting. Stellan plunked down cross-legged on the grass next to Madge and produced a lance from the leather satchel at his hip. Just as Norah was about to investigate, Madge hopped on Pepe's back and charged at Frondle's ankles with a whoop, lance out for kneecap-level jousting. Frondle parried that too, though Madge cut a slice through his cheerful silk.

When things quieted for a beat, Norah called everyone together.

"Thank you all for joining us to celebrate a new stage in Cleo's life. I look forward to seeing what she'll do next. However, I have an ulterior motive for bringing you here."

Expectant faces stared at her. Even Pepe paused, a chunk of Norah's rosemary plant dangling from his mouth. *So that's where my rosemary has been going.*

"I have located the Dark Hound server farm, and I am preparing to launch an assault. Those people are responsible for the deaths of many Silver Griffin agents, and they have powerful allies. It won't be safe, and I don't want anyone to feel pressured to join me. However, if you choose to help, I would be honored."

Someone in the crowd snorted, and Norah was offended for a half-second before realizing it was her mother.

"You hardly have to ask, dear." Petra tucked her arm through Lincoln's as they moved to stand behind her.

"I'm in." Andrew joined her. "And unless Quint wants a lifetime of wet willies, he'll help too."

"Hey!" Quint looked up from digging his burger pit in the middle of the lawn.

"I eagerly anticipate the fulfillment of my oath," Frondle replied.

"I'll bet you do," Madge muttered from atop Pepe. The pirate tattoo on Andrew's bicep waggled its eyebrows lasciviously. Norah flushed.

"I'm getting good at this jousting thing, so I'm in," Madge said. Pepe huffed and reared like a warhorse. His and Madge's faces were so ferocious that their silhouette looked intimidating. Norah wept for her enemies' kneecaps.

"I'll help," a voice added from under the lemon tree. It was Uriel. "I don't like my code being used for evil."

"If you'll have me, I'll join you," Castor offered.

"What are you going to do, Puppet Boy? Have a bear on a unicycle sing *The Great American Songbook* at them until they surrender?" Stellan muttered.

Castor puffed out his chest. "I've been working on a battle puppet."

Stellan's eyes narrowed. Norah looked at him with open pleading and held her breath until the wrinkle between his eyes softened. "You're doing a good turn for Cleo. Anyway, however bad you are, this Cook Forester is worse. Far be it from me to keep you off the front lines. Please, step in front of as many bullets as possible."

Castor nodded enthusiastically. "Thank you? Your beard looks, um, very impressive."

Stellan glared at Castor, tossed the red waves dramatically over his shoulder, and wandered toward Stan.

Norah nodded. Pulling out her wand, she tapped it against her phone. A large map of the Humpr offices appeared in the air above the courtyard.

"All right. Everyone's going to have a specific job…"

The battle planning took them well into the night. When she was done, Norah was unable to sleep and stared at the plaster on her ceiling. They would be taking down Dark Hound. She patted the empty space beside her and thought about Frondle.

Cook Forester doesn't stand a chance.

CHAPTER TWENTY-TWO

Norah attempted to adjust Frondle's armor, but its construction was complicated and she was unfamiliar with elven scalework, so she only succeeded in repeatedly poking him in the collarbone.

Stepping back, she admired him. "You should go clubbing in that some time." The gleaming scales rippled hypnotically over his chest.

"Are Los Angeles nightclubs frequently assaulted by evil forces?" Frondle asked.

"If you count bachelorette parties, yes."

The attack force had collected at a Denny's near the Humpr headquarters. Frondle was worried that they would be conspicuous, but Norah assured him that Denny's was used to much weirder sights in the middle of the night.

They split into the frontal and perimeter teams and headed to the building at staggered intervals. The last vehicle to leave was a big van Andrew's business used to transport the mobile tattoo setup. Jackie drove, and Uriel was in the back, surrounded by stacks of computer equipment they'd retrieved from a relieved Hazel earlier in the week.

Uriel had checked his gear like an anxious mother hen and declared it undamaged.

They parked a block away and continued on foot into the collection of walkways and ponds at the center of the complex. Once there, Norah turned on her radio magic and extended its reach into the building.

"There's a guard at the security station. There are three people upstairs, but they're not moving. Probably programming night owls." She sent the magic down into the building and gasped. "It's busy. Even busier than the last time I was here." She picked up her walkie-talkie. "I need everyone on their A-game. There's a sizeable night crew."

The walkie popped with a sea of acknowledgments. When everyone was in position, Norah nodded. Frondle raised his bow, the string of light crackling as he drew it. Norah gripped her wand in her right hand and pushed a button on her walkie with the left.

"Go!"

She couldn't see the resulting explosion of activity from her location. The fountains that fed the ponds burbled as she and Frondle raced across the cement toward the doors.

Norah grabbed the handle, praying Uriel's skills were as good as he claimed. It opened, and she breathed a sigh of relief.

"Hey!" A guard got to his feet in a small pool of light at the lobby security desk. Norah shot a crackling blue stun spell at him before the guard could say a second word. Frondle secured his arms and legs with enchanted zip-ties.

"Lobby is clear," Norah whispered into her walkie-talkie.

A faint crash came from high in the building. Wild clangs echoed down the stairwell, and then the door burst open. Cleo flapped into the room and alit on the security desk. In addition to the wings on her feet, a GoPro camera was strapped to her head. The source of the noise skittered in behind her.

The battle puppet shone a brilliant silver in the low light. It had six articulated titanium legs, each tapering to a deadly point. It resembled a lighthouse with a faceted bulb in the center. Everything appeared to be in good shape.

Castor jogged through the door, panting, and patted the battle puppet on one leg. "Good job, girl," he whispered.

Norah raised an eyebrow. "How'd the remote battle puppet operation go?"

"Um, they're all down? And not dead," he added. "It's harder if Cleo's spinning the camera around."

"I had to kick some programmers in the face," Cleo shot back defensively.

Hooves clicked on marble as Pepe trotted through the automatic doors, resplendent in a metal breastplate. Madge rode him, gripping a large shield of dwarven metal in one hand and her lance in the other.

"Let's go." Norah herded them into the elevator.

Uriel's voice crackled over the walkie. "An automated emergency alert went out, but I intercepted it. It's possible someone below saw it."

"Copy that." The elevator doors hissed shut, and they descended to Sub-basement Three.

Norah couldn't sense anyone in the hallway beyond but threw up a sheer blue shield just in case. The doors opened, but no one was outside.

She stepped into the hall. "Now's the time to live up to your name, UrbanWurm," she murmured into the handset. "Find us a way in."

"There's a cluster of firewalled code in one of the small rooms to your right," Uriel replied. "I think it's an elevator."

He directed her to a door a few paces down, which was one of the rooms she had checked on her previous visit. Her shoulders slumped as she scanned metal shelves stacked with old paint cans. Norah pushed a few around, but there was a wall behind them.

"Why would they keep empty paint cans?" Castor weighed one in his hand. They were all dry and useless.

"Everyone, stand back." Castor leaned down beside his spider puppet. "Fluffers, check for magic."

"You named your murder puppet 'Fluffers?'"

"I thought it would be less intimidating," Castor said. "Anyway, you know how magic leaves a trail but eventually disintegrates? I enchanted Fluffers to detect much smaller amounts than what witches and wizards can see with our magical sight. Fluffers sniffed out a glamour in Griffith Park a full month after I cast it."

They stepped back as Castor operated the battle puppet. His wand made barely detectable movements, and the tip of his tongue slipped into the corner of his mouth under a look of intense concentration. One of Fluffers's arms stretched toward an electric socket. Norah probed the spot with a wave of blue magic. Where had she felt similar power?

"The library!" she exclaimed.

"We don't have time to do book research," Frondle said gently.

"I recognize this. It's like the magic at the library, where there are hidden rooms full of spellbooks. There's a pocket of unreality here."

She narrowed her vision and investigated the pinprick of magic. It was a complicated spell, with many twists and turns woven into a minute area. Norah poked around until she found a loose edge, then pulled.

The wall shivered, and with an ominous creak, the outlet grew. The air distorted sickeningly as it stretched toward the ceiling and floor, making Frondle look like a cubist painting. Finally, the holes for the two prongs were the size of doors. As Norah was about to step into the one on the left, Castor grabbed her arm.

"That spell distorts the size of the outlet, but it's still electrified," he said. "Be careful. Try not to serve Cook any char-grilled witch."

Norah's organs dropped into weird places as she stepped into a new reality. A clearly marked plastic walkway led to an arch in the back. Norah shivered at the electrical buzz from above. Her stomach looped as she stepped through the distorted arch and re-entered conventional reality. The silver doors of an elevator gleamed on the other side of the small room.

Norah held up her walkie. "We're in. Let's go down." One by one, her crew came through the arch behind her.

This elevator ride was long, and Norah gripped her

wand as they descended into a hectic hive of activity. The sea of desires and emotions was mostly directed toward work tasks. Good.

Norah untangled the threads of emotions from below. At the end of the shaft were two bright balls of nervous anger—guards who were serious about their work and prepared to use violence. "The Welcome Wagon is expecting us."

Frondle, looking determined, nodded.

Cleo flapped up. "Stand to the sides. I'll fly out and draw their magical fire, and you can get them while they're distracted."

"Are you sure?" Norah didn't like the idea of the pixie taking so much heat. *She'd* never found a way through the cursed wood, but somebody else might.

"Unless you've developed impenetrable hex- and spell-proof wooden skin, then yeah, I'm sure," Cleo said.

Norah pressed against the side of the elevator as Cleo hovered at chest level. Frondle pressed against Norah. Even through the scales of his armor, she could feel his heat.

"Why isn't the door opening?" Castor whispered. Fluffers shivered.

"Are they blocking it from outside?" Norah whispered. Then she felt behind her. Her butt was pressing the Close Door button. "Oops." She moved a quarter-inch, and the doors opened.

Gunfire that sounded like thunder entered the elevator. Fluffers enclosed Castor in a protective but terrifying-looking hug. There were two loud thumps, a final spray of bullets, and then a small voice.

"That's Round One, I guess," Cleo said.

From behind a protective shield, Norah peeked out. The floor was covered in bullet casings, and Cleo was planted firmly on the chest of a body clad in black tactical armor. One of the leather straps on her wooden shoes dangled around the ankle, smoking where a bullet cut through it.

Norah sent a quick repair spell into the leather harness. "Are they dead?"

"No." Cleo tested the strap. "I hit 'em with my flat side. If you want 'em dead, I can use a corner."

"No thanks." Norah secured the guards' hands with multiple reinforced zip-ties.

A long hall stretched toward a pair of double doors.

"Something's off." Norah stepped forward to investigate.

"Stop," Uriel commanded. "There's a laser detection system."

Frondle closed his eyes. The hall was crisscrossed by glowing thin red beams in an intricate web.

"Let me down." Madge's voice was gravelly.

Pepe sat. She clambered off, then dropped to her stomach and looked down the length of the marble floor below the laser beams.

"I can get through." Before anyone could stop her, she Army-crawled down the hall. "You know, it's kind of insulting," she shouted over her shoulder. "Security systems never account for small beings like pixies or fairies or rodent shifters. With a little ingenuity, we could walk out of Fort Knox."

Norah envisioned Madge sashaying out of Fort Knox in

MARTHA CARR & MICHAEL ANDERLE

a pair of red velvet boots, half-crushed by the weight of a gold bar. She snorted.

"What?" Frondle asked.

Norah shook her head.

"I'm in." Madge rose to her feet at the far end of the hall. "Where do I go?"

Uriel's voice crackled. "There should be a panel. I can get you the code, but you'll have to punch it in manually."

Madge cursed as she craned her neck at a panel four feet off the ground. She clambered onto the baseboard, testing a foothold, but slid back down.

"Wait," Norah said quietly. "Step to your left about two feet. I need a clear shot."

She dropped onto her stomach, aimed, and fired a thin line of blue antigrav magic across the marble. Madge intercepted it. The pixie's hair floated around her in a cloud as she pulled herself up the wall like an astronaut.

Uriel read her the code, and the laser beams vanished. Norah strode down the hall, with Frondle's scaled armor clinking comfortingly behind her. Pepe trotted to Madge, the jousting lance clutched delicately between his teeth, and kneeled so she could clamber onto his back.

"Thanks." Madge politely ignored the goat spit on her silver weapon.

"Nice work, cavalry," Norah said. Pepe's teeth spread over his lips in a goaty smile. A leaf fragment from Norah's rosemary plant was stuck between two yellowed molars.

"Let's go," she continued. She sensed two guard stations behind the heavy double doors and many people beyond.

She drew her wand in a circle. A disk of transparent

blue magic shimmered before her as she flung the door open.

The force of the magical blast from the other side shattered the blue shield and sent her sliding back. She found her footing and stumbled through the open door as a sallow witch with greasy hair raised her staff.

Norah's wand was like a nail clipper next to a chainsaw. The staff was six feet long and intricately carved with demonic figures and runes to inflict pain and injury. Startling red-and-black tattoos crawled up the witch's cheeks.

The witch set the staff on the ground, vaulted on top of a security desk, and fired a vicious ball of putrid orange energy at Norah's face. Norah ducked, realizing with a sickening feeling that Frondle was behind her.

He swung a net of woven gold beams that he held to his side like a toreador to capture the blast, then flung the magic back at the staff-wielder before the orange flames corroded the net. Their attacker caught the ball in the middle of her staff, and a fist-sized chunk of tiger's eye embedded in the wood absorbed it.

She's using it as a magical battery. Neat trick.

Frondle loosed three quick arrows, bowstring thrumming, as Norah turned toward the ball of emotion from the other guard. It took a few passes of her radio magic to find the fairy, and when she saw him, she struggled not to laugh. His startlingly pink wings, shot through with pearlescent veins, were straight out of a five-year-old girl's bedroom. His face was impossibly beautiful, like a ceramic doll's. As he zipped past, he left more pink glitter in the air than a dancer from Jumbo's Clown Room.

"You got a problem, witch?" he asked in a disconcertingly deep voice, raising a miniscule pistol. It was tiny and adorable, like an accessory for Militia Barbie. Norah forgot to be afraid of it until a rice-grain-sized bullet struck the webbing between two of her fingers.

"Ow!" A drop of blood welled from the wound. She was about to dismiss it as an annoyance when penetrating cold bloomed at the site. The droplet of blood froze solid, and white lines shot from it like cracking ice.

"Fuck!" Norah barely managed to grab her wand with her left hand before it fell out of her lifeless fingers. She shot a clumsy left-handed warming spell into her arm and screamed as warring hot-and-cold needles shot through her flesh.

She fired a stunning spell at the fairy as he aimed between Frondle's eyes. The fairy ducked the spell, and the microbullet went wide.

The witch whirled the staff and sent a rain of glowing splinters into the room. Norah blocked them with a haphazard shield, and Frondle dove in front of Pepe and Madge, the magic sliding off his armor like toothpicks. He raised his vambrace over his face to block two more incoming pink bullets, but the third slipped into the gap between armor and helmet. The light elf bellowed in pain and dropped.

"Pick on someone your own size!" Madge shouted. She spurred Pepe, and he hopped over Frondle's prone form, then wound up for a soaring leap that brought them level with the fairy. Madge threw her lance with a berserker's scream, and it bit into one gossamer wing. The tip crunched into the far wall, pinning the fairy to the plaster like a butterfly.

Cleo dove at the witch with the staff. When the witch's first three spells failed to connect with the flying rune-etched cube, she cursed and batted at Cleo as if she were an obstinate *piñata*. Seeing her fellow guard pinned to the wall, she took a final screaming swing and sent Cleo crashing into the security desk.

"Trigger the cage!" she shouted. The fairy fired a bolt of magic into a glowing sphere at the center of the ceiling, which Norah had assumed was a light fixture, then grunted and shot the orb with a bullet. As it pinged, a dome of rust-colored magic dropped from the ceiling with a massive scraping noise, trapping them underneath. Norah hit it with a bolt of blue magic, but it ricocheted and slid off the frozen Frondle's boots.

While an aggravated Pepe kicked at the magical dome, Norah stooped beside Frondle. His face was pale marble, expressionless and colorless. She cursed as she probed with thin tendrils of blue eucalyptus magic. She had to work swiftly to reverse the freezing spell.

She conjured warming blue light and sent it through Frondle's arteries to distribute heat to his face and brain. When Frondle's eyes widened in pain, she felt simultaneous relief and guilt. He was conscious, but thawing out wasn't going to be pleasant.

She gripped one of his gloved hands and continued the spell, keeping one ear open as Madge, Pepe, and Castor's gleaming spiderbot pounded the magical trap. The witch with the staff unpinned the pink fairy from the wall as a new figure entered the room.

The man was of average height and had brown hair. He wore a charcoal-colored sweatshirt emblazoned with

Humpr's H logo. Norah recognized him from the headshot on his company's website.

"Hello, Cook," she said.

A lithe figure was at his side. The paint on her arm was gone, and the gold gleamed a buttery yellow except for her nails, which were tipped with razor-sharp titanium. Radio magic confirmed that the woman was burning mad and out for revenge.

"It's impressive that you made it this far." The CEO sneered. "The magic I understand, but tell me how you disabled my surveillance cameras? I have the best digital security money can buy."

Norah's walkie-talkie crackled, and Uriel answered. "That's not true. I'm the best there is, and I'm not very interested in money."

"Is that the Wurm?" Cook looked impressed and wary. Behind him, golden light danced as Sedona flexed her fingers.

"You lied to me about Dark Hound," Uriel added.

"Hey, don't blame me for failing to answer questions you never bothered to ask." Cook rolled his eyes. "Let's cut a deal. If you walk me through my system's exploitable weaknesses, I'll kill your friends super-duper fast. I'm talking quantum-computing speeds. Or, keep your mouth shut, and I'll go slow. Analog. DMV speed."

Silence from the walkie-talkie. Norah raised an eyebrow. "You're not going to kill us."

Cook waved a dismissive hand. "Your ragtag assault team is cute, but you'll never get out of that cage. My teams of skilled wizards worked on it for three weeks. You might be scrappy, but you're not bright. We've been monitoring your walkie-talkie communications since you went through the socket. All we had to do was herd you in here and spring the mousetrap."

Static crackled through the walkie-talkie, cloaking a faint pattern of taps and dashes. Norah knew it by heart. She grinned. "Yeah, maybe, but you're overlooking a huge problem."

Cook scoffed. "What's that?"

The room shook, and a hairline fracture raced across the floor under the CEO's feet. He shied away as it widened. With another colossal rumble, the floor bulged.

Norah grinned as the magical cage deflected the plaster raining from the ceiling. "Your problem is that we're not the main attack force."

Thunder filled the room as a spiraling metal tip burst through the floor, spinning like an unrestrained firehose. Sedona used her elemental powers to grip the drill and the spinning ground to a halt, but it was too late. A mini-submarine burst into the room behind it.

"Execute Operation Flashbulb!" Norah clamped her eyes shut.

The lighthouse-style fixture on Fluffers' body ratcheted out and discharged a retina-burning flash of magical light with a resounding *click*.

A beep from the spiderbot told them the coast was clear. Norah opened her eyes as a hatch on the metal drill cylinder hissed. Petra, Lincoln, Andrew, and Quint tumbled out, wands aloft. Behind them, Stellan poked into view, wearing sleek white protective goggles. His luxurious beard was swept to the side in a fetching French braid.

Their enemy was thrown into chaos. The fairy, flying

blind, slammed into the side of the magical cage. The witch with the staff screamed and raked at her eyes. Petra shot a stunning spell at her, and Andrew scooped the struggling fairy into his enchanted net. The fairy's shrieked obscenities suggested he perform anatomical impossibilities. The rest of the bad guys were stunned into silence.

As her mother and father disabled the glowing orb and set her attack team free, Norah searched the room. Cook and Sedona were gone.

Norah jabbed the net, shedding clouds of pink glitter. "How many security people are left?"

The fairy spat a glob of opalescent goo on Norah's black-clad leg. She nodded at Andrew, who shook the bag.

"Sedona was the last one," the fairy snarled. "She stays with Cook."

"Where is Cook?"

The fairy closed his mouth.

"Shake and bake him," she told Andrew.

"He'll kill me!" The fairy clung miserably to the net.

"Tell us where Cook is, and we'll make sure he won't hurt you or anyone else." Norah made her voice sound menacing.

The fairy sighed. "He has a safe room in his office off the server farm. There's a hatch under his polar bear rug."

"Polar bears are endangered," Petra snapped.

"I'm not the one who shot it." The fairy collapsed dramatically at the bottom of the net bag.

Norah sent her radio magic into the next room. At last, the server farm. The human activity beyond the doors was ordinary.

"Uriel, work your magic," Norah said into her walkie.

"No magic here, just straight hacking," Uriel replied. After a moment, the fire alarm shrieked, and the emergency exit signs glowed chartreuse.

"Hide or glamour yourselves," Norah shouted.

Pepe and Madge ducked behind the desk. Norah hustled to the corner and cast a rough-and-ready glamour to look like a small but smoky fire. Seconds later, workers burst through the doors toward the stairs, screaming as they sprinted past Norah's flames.

"Why aren't the sprinklers going off?" one shouted.

"Sorry about this." Uriel said, and the overhead sprinklers went off. Norah shivered under the spray. The workers ran faster, and a minute later, Norah sensed that the server farm was empty.

Stellan sauntered to the drill rig and pulled out an enormous gleaming axe. "I don't know about you, but I'm ready to hack into the system."

Inspired by the dwarf, Norah grabbed the double-ended staff from the stunned guard witch, testing a twirl. The tiger's eye pulsed with energy, and Norah used it to recharge her magical reserves.

Petra pulled a heavy, wriggling sack from the depths of the drill.

"How did they handle the journey?" Norah asked.

Petra shrugged. "It was warm in there, but we're not too crispy." A ferocious shriek filtered through the heavy fabric.

Norah's plan was uncomplicated: cause chaos and destruction. If cooling was important for the servers, indiscriminate immolation from Petra's bag of mature draconewts would be an effective counter.

They pushed through the final doors. The blinking lights of the server racks stretched in rows across the cavernous concrete room. Cables spilled like guts from the metal servers, winding into huge ropes that snaked across the ceiling.

Staring at the place that had caused so much misery, Norah raised the end of the staff she judged to be the more destructive. "Playtime, everyone. Do your worst." Rolling the shaft between her fingers, she selected a server cage forty feet away, drew a sizeable pulse of energy into the tip, and fired a blast that turned the stack to glittering mist.

The crowd behind her let out an enormous whoop and went to work. Stellan, wisely wearing his goggles, swung his mighty axe and split a server like a log. Sparks flew, and the debris hummed dangerously.

"Don't get electrocuted more times than I can heal you." Norah twirled the destruction staff and swung it like a baseball bat at a cooling tube. Fluid splashed on the floor, and the lights on the nearby stack blinked a rapid, comforting red.

"Give me one second to cut the electricity," Uriel said. The lights on the servers went dead.

"Woohoo!" Madge shouted as Pepe reared and punched a sharp hoof into the nearest server.

"Care to play doubles demolition, dear?" Petra asked, patting Lincoln's arm.

Norah's father grinned and pointed his wand at a server. As it levitated, a fireball crackled from Petra's wand. The metal exploded in a rain of shards.

"Nice." Andrew smirked at Quint. "I bet I can destroy more servers than you."

Quint snorted. "Yeah, right." Wand out, he cast a magical dome over an entire row of stacks. After a moment, the metal boxes glowed red-hot, and the connecting cables melted.

"I use this spell to heat my lattes," Quint explained.

Frondle walked purposefully down one aisle, elven daggers cutting zigzagging lines through metal and cables. His armor glittered under the emergency lights and sparks.

Norah ran after him and grabbed his arm. "Let's go find Cook."

Looking morose, Frondle wiped a blob of circuit board off his dagger and fell in behind her. After a minute, they located Cook's office in an alcove near the north end.

The interior design was so clichéd that Norah was embarrassed. A broad expanse of mahogany desk reflected an Edison bulb that lit a menagerie of hunting trophies. Norah pulled leather-bound books off the shelves and found them to be mere decorations. The one real treasure was a bottle of Talisker 25 she found in a desk drawer and moved to her backpack.

Zipping it shut, she found Frondle standing still, staring at a leather Chesterfield sofa along one wall. His face was flushed, and there was a contemplative look in his eyes. Norah did not need her radio magic to follow his thinking.

We could reasonably conclude that Dark Hound has been destroyed and our oaths have been fulfilled. The leather looked very soft.

Norah shook her head to clear it. Business first, pleasure later. She moved the polar bear rug aside to find a large portal but no visible lock.

"Hey, Uriel. Any chance you can pop this open?" she asked.

"I'm not picking up any electrical signals," Uriel replied. "The safe room must be isolated from the rest of the building."

Frondle, not interested in waiting, drove his left dagger into the metal and winced when the point bounced off without a scratch. "That's dark elf construction. It'll take months to cut through it."

Norah shrugged. "Hey!" she shouted at the portal. "We're going to bring this building down around your heads. Your food and water and *Rick and Morty* DVDs won't last forever. Unless you want to starve to death underground, you better open up."

After a moment, the door slid back with a hiss. Norah grasped her wand, but the scene inside wasn't the last stand she expected.

Cook Forester's safe room looked like a divorced father's apartment. It had two bunk beds, shelves full of canned food, and a big-screen TV on the wall. A groan of pain came from Cook, who was draped across a sofa. His face was yellow, and a rusty stain spread across the floor. The onyx hilt of a dagger protruded from between his ribs.

A rug had been flung aside, and the black maw of an open hatch gaped. A draft blew a strand of Norah's hair across her eyes.

"An escape hatch."

Frondle peered into the depths as she climbed down the ladder. "Who stabbed you?"

Cook's head tilted toward Norah. He wheezed,

"Domenico. He was working with Sedona, the traitor. They escaped."

"Domenico is here?"

Cook exhaled sharply and half-laughed, then his eyes slid to the escape tunnel. "Not anymore." His eyes lost focus.

Norah shot a healing spell into Cook's body, but he screamed, and the magic dissolved. His body was fighting the magic. After two more tries, she concentrated her energy, looking at minute traces of his blood.

Norah gasped when she realized what was going on. Cook's blood was full of microscopic antimagic wells. More were pouring out of the tip of the onyx dagger. It was a grim way of making sure your downed enemies stayed down. A healing spell would dissipate in seconds.

"That's dark elf construction." Frondle ran one fingertip across the blade. She couldn't heal Cook until she figured out a way to clean his blood, but he was almost out of time.

Norah blinked. "Do we have that fairy's freeze gun?"

Frondle scaled the ladder. Norah heard deep-voiced shouts, then he dropped back in, rubbing a bite on one finger. "Never underestimate the pink ones." He handed her the gun. "Don't you think he's been injured enough?"

Cook's face grew paler as Norah pointed the gun at his forehead.

"Have you ever heard of cryogenic freezing?" she asked. "If we freeze his tissue, what happens in his blood won't matter. It'll stabilize him until we can get help."

"Will that work?"

Desperation edged her voice. "Maybe."

"Wait," Cook wheezed. "Domenico. Traitor. Stabbed me.

Ran away with Sedona. I injected him with a tracker. A while ago. I thought this might happen."

"How'd you convince a Mafia don to let you inject him with a tracker?"

Cook wheezed. "Said it was a nootropic vitamin shot." He waved his fingers at a chrome receiver on the floor with a digital map on the screen. There was a blinking dot representing the receiver and one for the tracker, which was headed toward the ocean.

"Thanks." She pulled the tiny gun's trigger.

The bullet hit him between the eyes. Norah put two more shots into his chest and stomach. He was an icicle in seconds. After testing to see that his flesh was firm, she removed the dagger, shuddering when she touched his frozen skin.

"Watch him," she directed Frondle as she climbed the ladder.

At the server farm, she dodged a belch of fire from a draconewt that was nesting inside a busted server.

"I let them out a few minutes ago," Petra said. "They've been satisfyingly destructive." Bursts of orange fire and smoke rolled throughout the space.

Norah sighed. "I found Cook, but I don't know if he's going to survive." Using a scarcity of words that would have made Ernest Hemingway proud, she explained what she'd found in Cook's office, aside from the Talisker. "We should go out the back door."

"I've gotta take the drill rig back the way we came," Stellan told her. "I borrowed it from my mother. If I don't give it back, she'll shave my beard off." He placed a protective calloused hand over the French braid dangling from his chin.

"It would be the world's loss. Can you get all the prisoners out?"

"It might be a bit of a sardine can back there, but aye. I won't leave them in the rubble." Stellan saluted and strode away.

Norah took a deep breath as Quint and Andrew jostled through the door to Cook's office, shooting blasts of explosive magic in all directions. She pulled the final package out of her backpack, the last piece of the puzzle in Operation Burn It All Down. Crouching, she placed a plastic flowerpot, a bright green seed, a small bag of soil, and a vial of tears that she, Frondle, and several onions had generated the day before on the floor. She wasn't taking any chances.

Yolen had supported the demolition effort by donating a spare magic bean. After emptying the soil into the pot and pushing in the seed, Norah watered it with tears and waited.

When the first green shoot unwound from the soil, Norah sprinted to Cook's office, bringing up the rear. She followed her brothers through the escape hatch, the tunnel walls creaking as roots shot into the earth.

The climb to the surface was long. What had been an easy elevator ride down was a forearm-burning haul back up as her family traded off casting antigrav spells on Cook's frozen body.

As Norah's exhaustion grew, so did her anger at Domenico's escape. Every few minutes, she checked the tracker. He was moving slowly, probably on foot, heading south to the coast. She resisted the urge to shout at her mother to move faster. All those times as a kid when she'd dragged her feet getting out of the house were now haunting her.

When they punched out a manhole in the street a few blocks away, Norah realized they might still have a chance.

"Take care of Cook," she said. "Frondle and I are going after Domenico."

The light elf gave a stiff, shallow bow, and they sprinted to her car.

CHAPTER TWENTY-THREE

Norah wished she owned a boat. Before, she'd considered watercraft a frivolous means of siphoning money from the rich. Now, as Domenico's dot moved into the blue expanse of the Pacific, she reconsidered. Hopping the fence onto the docks was easy, but as they ran across the floating walkways, Norah was at a loss. They could jump aboard any boat, but operating it was a different matter.

Then she spotted a silver-haired man pulling a gleaming speedboat out of a slip. "Go!" she screamed at Frondle, pointing. The elven armor became an incandescent streak as Frondle ran at top speed and leapt onto the craft. There was enough light on the docks for him to lasso the silver-haired man with thin tendrils. His efforts were rewarded with shouting and thrashing.

The boat drifted into open water. The gap between the gunwale and docks was at the limit of the distance Norah could leap with an antigrav boost.

She poured physical energy into her quads and magical

energy into her sneakers as she sprang into the air. Time slowed as her right leg stretched toward the polished honey-colored wood of the speedboat. *Fuck.* She was going to miss it by a foot.

As her arms windmilled, Frondle reached out and pulled her to safety, and she tumbled into his arms. She brushed a lock of golden hair out of his eye, and his hand cupped her side.

"Hey! No funny business in the boat! You two are too old to be joyriding and making out," a gruff voice said. The boat's owner was struggling in the bow, gold light binding him tighter as he thrashed. He was right.

Norah rolled off Frondle and popped to her feet. "Have you ever steered a boat?"

Frondle shook his head. "Have you?"

Norah grabbed the throttle. "I went kayaking in a lake at summer camp when I was twelve."

"Was it a good experience?"

"I fell out and lost a flip-flop." She pressed the throttle forward. The boat jumped in the water, and she handed the tracker to Frondle. Domenico's dot was miles away, west of Santa Catalina Island, and it had stopped moving.

Norah shivered in the cold, and Frondle frowned at the receiver. "Are we being pursued? Is that why we're zigzagging so much?" The boat jolted in the water again.

Norah gritted her teeth and tried to smooth their course. She was too tired to appreciate the first threads of morning light rising behind them, but the warmth stopped her shivering. Frondle wrapped an arm around her shoulder as she cast a warming spell on their prisoner, who had gone silent on the bottom of the boat.

"This isn't a joyride, is it?"

"No."

"I do feel a certain amount of joy at burnishing the tarnish off an unfulfilled oath," Frondle said somberly.

"That better not be a euphemism." The man grunted as he wiggled into a sitting position. "Where are we going?"

Norah shaded her eyes with one hand and waved vaguely at the empty horizon, her stomach sinking.

"We're getting close," Frondle said some time later.

Norah snatched the tracker. Their dot was practically on top of the tracking device. If Domenico was on a boat, it should have been right in front of them, but there was only water and air and sky.

Norah looked ahead with magical sight, hoping to see a boat-sized invisibility spell. No luck. She squinted at the tracker. Was it her imagination, or was Domenico moving? Yes! It was faint, but it was there.

"He must have found a way to get rid of the tracker and thrown it overboard," Frondle said.

"Maybe." Norah sent her radio magic deep into the gray-green ocean. She felt pulses of consciousness from the life below: fish big and small, and what she was sure was a whale. She smiled at the peaceful waves of emotion from the big mammal and extended her range to its farthest limits. No humans. If by some miracle Domenico was underwater, he was out of range.

Pulling out her phone, Norah navigated to the Dark Hound website. Only an error screen loaded. She showed it to Frondle. "We have to keep looking for Domenico. I can't let him get away with killing Silver Griffin agents."

Frondle nodded somberly, and she grabbed his hand.

Sunrise cast a buttery light on his gorgeous face. "In the meantime, however, we have some celebrating to do. Let's go home."

The speed at which Frondle ran to the wheel and sped toward shore was very romantic.

Norah sat by the boat's owner. "I hope there's some way we can apologize for, um, commandeering your boat. Without involving the authorities."

"Piracy is a felony."

"Okay, but wouldn't you prefer money to entanglement in maritime law?" Norah asked.

"Check my pockets," Frondle said.

Norah raised a jaunty eyebrow and slid an arm around him, then pulled out a ruby the size of a robin's egg. Frondle stared at it wanly.

"That's my good luck charm. I dropped it once at acting class. Madame Ploot said I should put it in a bank, but I don't think banks need more luck."

"Damn straight," the boat owner interjected.

"Are you sure? We might be overshooting the target," Norah whispered.

Frondle nodded. "You're my luck now, Norah."

He waved his fingers, and the gold light unwound from the boat owner. He scrambled warily to his feet, and Norah held out the ruby. "Will this do?"

The ruby disappeared into the man's pocket, and he narrowed his eyes. "Why don't I take you to the dock before Mr. Pointy Ears blows the engine." He stormed to the wheel.

Lincoln met them at the dock, and Norah's nerves lit when she saw that Petra wasn't with him.

"They went back to Andrew's," Lincoln said. "I wanted to ask for your help dealing with Cook. I'm taking him to a healer I know. A grand potionmaster."

"Why me?" Norah realized she sounded like a teenager who'd been asked to do the dishes. Her plans had not included running an extra errand with her father.

Lincoln looked at the ocean. "Well, this healer and I have a history. She's an old flame."

Norah's eyes widened. "Dad! Do you need help with your ex-girlfriend?"

"Um…"

Frondle shifted in his armor, and he patted her arm. "You must help your father in his hour of need. I should get some sleep. I'm due on set in…" he eyed the position of the sun in the sky, "three hours."

"You're shooting today?"

"Reshoots."

Norah sighed and drove him to his car, promising to see him later.

CHAPTER TWENTY-FOUR

Since Lincoln said his ex was a grand potionmaster, Norah had assumed they would be heading to Topanga or Ojai. Instead, Lincoln drove them to the heart of Hollywood's clubbing district. He pulled into an alley behind a club whose sign read THE CAULDRON. The U in CAULDRON was an upside-down, a pointy witch's hat. Norah narrowed her eyes.

"She's from a different generation." Lincoln had noticed Norah's disdain for the classic witch iconography. "I'm told the club is groovy. They play deep-house music and up-and-coming siren classics."

"What do you know about deep-house music?" Norah asked, laughing.

"I taste-test what the kids are listening to," Lincoln said. "Our farmhand plays weird stuff."

They carried Cook's frozen body through the back door. Exhausted, Norah cast a shoddy glamour to make him look like an amplifier.

The witch who met them at the bar of the empty nightclub was a dead ringer for Stevie Nicks. She wore a pointy black hat that draped elegantly to the side, made of what Norah guessed was cashmere. The witch's eyes grazed Norah and landed on Lincoln with a simmering bloom of warmth.

"Linky! You're looking well," she drawled. "Care for some absinthe?"

Lincoln snuck a look at his watch. It was 7:30 in the morning. "Raincheck?" They hauled Cook onto the bar, and Lincoln unwrapped the dagger from a length of black silk.

Esmee stroked the hilt with the tip of a black lace glove. "I've only seen its equal in the Silver Griffin vaults. A nasty weapon to kill the unkillable from an old dark elf family. Freezing him was an interesting idea."

"It was the best I could do," Norah said apologetically.

"That wasn't meant as criticism. I'll do my best. It'll be nice to use the deep freezer for something other than making ice molds."

"Thanks," Lincoln said.

Esmee squeezed his hand with more familiarity than Norah was comfortable with. "You have nearly limitless credit here. Come back when the club is open. Gnomo's spinning next weekend."

"Ooh!" Norah said. The gnome deejay was gaining quite a reputation among her musically oriented peers.

"My clubbing days are behind me," Lincoln said.

"A great loss to the dance floor." Esmee tilted her head toward Norah. "Your father was the disco king in his day."

Norah's eyebrows shot into an area somewhere near the North Pole.

"Thanks, Esmee. Let me know if you need anything." Lincoln pulled his hand away.

As they clambered back in his car, Norah failed to contain her laughter. "'*Linky?*' Linky the disco king?"

"If you stop laughing, I'll buy you breakfast."

"I'll go hungry, thanks." Norah couldn't stop chuckling.

"Ugh. Fine. I'll buy you breakfast anyway. What do you want?"

"Huge volumes of bacon. And pie. Can you get bacon pie in Los Angeles?"

"That's my girl. You know, I'm very proud of you, sweetheart."

"I let Domenico get away." Norah glanced at the tracker. Domenico's dot was still in the ocean.

"We'll find him." Lincoln's voice was dark. "Trash always floats to the top."

As they pulled into the restaurant, the thin line of a beanstalk appeared in the sky to the west. The morning light reflected off its spreading emerald tendrils.

New life. Whether it was good or bad remained to be seen.

Get sneak peeks, exclusive giveaways, behind the scenes content, and more. PLUS you'll be notified of special **one day only fan pricing** on new releases.

Sign up today to get free stories.

Visit: https://marthacarr.com/read-free-stories/

I've started a project answering questions for my son about my life. I realized after last year's fifth round of cancer, and then chemo this time that he was expecting me to die sooner rather than later. It's been a lot for him to deal with and there isn't much I can do to make it better, except tell him stories that I can leave behind – eventually. Hopefully, a long time from now. I'm going to let you guys listen in as well.

My author notes for this year are going to be answers to questions and all of you can get to know me better, too. Maybe inspire, maybe give you a laugh along the way.

Today's question is: What were you like when you were thirty?

Turning thirty was probably the most seminal moment in my life that no one else noticed but me. Others might pick out when you were born, or when I met Michael and started Oriceran, or when cancer struck, but it was when I turned thirty. Everything changed forever.

That was the year I got divorced and had tiny you to take care of and an entire life ahead of me. I looked at how things had turned out trying to do things the way everyone else wanted and noticed the results. It was in that moment with very little left to lose that I finally found the courage to start charting a different course.

I declared myself a writer and set out to figure out what that meant, exactly.

By the way, this is also where everyone started to vehemently disagree with me about my choices. That never let up until I moved far enough away to not hear it anymore. I suppose if they're paying attention to my success, some minds may have changed. The biggest benefit from all the blathering and opining is that I learned to ask myself over time what I wanted and head for that.

Anyway, back to turning thirty.

I was newly single and had a newborn and had gotten myself hired as a reporter at the Charlottesville, Virginia daily newspaper. It was back when fax machines were a hot new invention and used that heat-treated paper that just rolled continuously out of the machine. Computers were fairly new on the scene, and you still had to explain to people how to go to a web site. Flip phones were all the rage.

I was full of mountain-size doubts, wondering what I was doing but this time I wasn't turning around, backing up or changing my mind. I just kept quietly going forward on this path I chose, no matter what other people said, all the time, about what I should be doing. Oh, the 'shoulds'.

I was also busy writing my first novel, a thriller

called *Wired* that I had started when I was still married. It would go on to be a pretty good seller, bought by almost every library system in the country and produced long lines at bookstores to see me. Some of those signings you came to with me in your stroller.

I asked so many questions of everyone I could find, and read every book on writing, attended seminars, went to writer retreats, created a writing group. Anything to help me get to that goal. The goal, though, I wasn't as clear about because I was making the mistake of shaping my goal as an answer to all the negative feedback.

Instead, the goal needed to be independent of outside blather. That would take me so many years to understand, but when I did, it finally brought me so much peace and ironically, success.

Thirty was the year I started living my life from a conscious place, instead of as a group afterthought.

Now, here I am at 63, more than double that age and the view from here is perfect. Thank goodness, all those years ago I stepped out into the life I wanted. I look back at all the pieces, all the things I've created - a national column, being a stringer for the Washington Post, publishing pieces in almost every major news outlet, on talk shows, researching a book on US orphanages, and now writing urban fantasy and I can see how the pieces make up an entire picture. And in the center of it, there's you. I hope my example of stubbornly sticking to my guns has helped you on your path in the music industry. Always be yourself, it works out in the long run and when you get toward the end of things, you'll see what a great ride it's been all along. Not that I'm done yet. I'm out here creating some new adventures for myself, even now. That Kickstarter in May for the new book is up next. Other things are busy percolating in my brain. Can't wait to get to them. May the same always be true for you. Love you. Love, Mom. More adventures to follow.

AUTHOR NOTES - MICHAEL ANDERLE

JANUARY 24, 2023

Thank you for not only reading this book but these author notes as well!

Lately, I've been talking about food in my author notes. During the winter months, it is on my mind as something to look forward to that has nothing to do with the cold.

The bone…chilling…cold. Mind you, I live in Las Vegas, so for me "bone-chilling cold" is when it is in the thirties and forties at night. For those living in a colder climate, that's "Get the Hell Out" cold.

TACO BELL

As an urban fantasy writer, my days are filled with the magical and mystical, but when it comes to fuel for my imagination and cold days and nights, there's nothing quite like the fiery, bold flavors of Taco Bell. As someone who is constantly typing on my keyboard, I often find myself too busy to cook, which is why I'm so grateful for this fast-food treasure trove of deliciousness.

One of the many things I love about Taco Bell is the

sheer variety of menu options available. Whether I'm craving a classic taco or a more innovative creation like the Chili-Cheese Burrito (BRING IT BACK!), there's always something new to discover.

What really sets Taco Bell apart, in my opinion, is the restaurant's *fearless approach* to flavor. While other fast-food chains play it safe, Taco Bell isn't afraid to go bold with spices and ingredients, which is music to the ears (and taste buds) of someone like me, who thrives on heat. And with a wide range of sauces to choose from, I can tailor my order to my personal taste preferences.

I'm a Medium and Hot guy. Occasionally, I'll just mild it and move on, but I like the zest.

Let's not forget about the prices, which are oh-so-friendly to a writer's budget. With so many menu items coming in under $5, I can indulge in my Taco Bell cravings without breaking the bank. Plus, with late-night hours, it's the perfect spot for a satisfying meal after a long writing session.

I just have to look out for my belt-line.

All in all, Taco Bell is a staple in the diet of this Urban Fantasy writer. The bold flavors, variety, and affordability make it a go-to choice for me, providing not just fuel for my body but also for my imagination.

Huh. I wonder if I write snarkier dialogue when I'm eating food from The Bell?

Chat with you in the next book.

Ad Aeternitatem,

Michael Anderle

MORE STORIES with Michael newsletter HERE: https://michael.beehiiv.com/

OTHER SERIES IN THE ORICERAN UNIVERSE:

CONNECT WITH THE AUTHORS

Martha Carr Social

Website: http://www.marthacarr.com

Facebook: https://www.facebook.com/groups/
MarthaCarrFans/

Michael Anderle Social

Website: http://lmbpn.com

Email List: http://lmbpn.com/email/

https://www.facebook.com/LMBPNPublishing

https://twitter.com/MichaelAnderle

https://www.instagram.com/lmbpn_publishing/

https://www.bookbub.com/authors/michael-anderle

BOOKS BY MICHAEL ANDERLE

Sign up for the LMBPN email list to be notified of new releases and special deals!

https://lmbpn.com/email/

For a complete list of books by Michael Anderle, please visit:

www.lmbpn.com/ma-books/

Printed in Great Britain
by Amazon